PRAISE FOR *NANCY*

"An alarming, beautifully compassionate novel. Original and perfect for these strange times we live in." — **Jazmina Barrera, author of** *On Lighthouses*

"'After a while, their silence is worse than being at death's door. Maybe even worse than hope,' says the protagonist of this beautiful, terrifying novel, which at times recalls César Vallejo's poems, at times Robert Browning's dramatic monologues, and at times Herta Müller's ferocious fiction. A single, simple special effect—pages sown with *X*s, stained with crosses—transforms the reading into an incessant, painful blinking. Readers vacillate, shift position, try out obvious or sophisticated or whimsical interpretations, and are as mistrustful of these tricks as Nancy herself would be of strangers who suddenly seem too interested in listening to her. An inventory of abandonment and abuse, inevitable diary of death and of growing up, a diatribe against routine religious fervor, and a bitter collection of involuntary poetry, this extraordinary novel far transcends denunciation and the exercise in style, reaching a new, unexpected, dissident realism."
— **Alejandro Zambra, author of** *Multiple Choice*

"A devastating, psychic exploration of our crumbling world, told in a visceral style that proves Bruno Lloret to be a force among the emerging Chilean writers of today."

— **Fernando A. Flores, author of**
Tears of the Trufflepig

"Bruno Lloret's *Nancy* is a requiem, a funeral pyre, a poetic novel dedicated to the factory towns and their unremembered inhabitants. Told with breathless economy, an entire world of Romany and gringos, sinners and the devout walk across the serrated desert of this Chilean masterpiece. Part coming-of-age, part meditation on poverty, grief, and environmental collapse, I've never read anything quite like it."

— **Mark Haber, author of** *Reinhardt's Garden*

"A moving, masterful debut... Death, trauma, violence, sexuality, family, religion, class, *Nancy*, in offering a tale of one, juxtaposes the individual's singularity with the similarity of shared human experience. With sparse prose and uncanny realism, Lloret thrusts the reader into a staccato reminiscence of a life spent in struggle and defeat. *Nancy* resonates; *Nancy* eulogizes; *Nancy* dignifies—perhaps most of all, *Nancy* empathizes, with and for a life, however fictional, that seldom enjoyed the grace it so quietly deserved."

— **Jeremy Garber, Powell's (Portland, OR)**

"A profound and disturbing meditation on the nature of belief, poverty and the human detritus of global capital." — *The Saturday Paper*

"*Nancy* is a work of great emotional and intellectual maturity. It is surprising that it is a debut novel. With it, Bruno Lloret announces himself as a writer who is unafraid to explore life at the margins of society, but who is sensitive to the complexity of his subject. The stark, brutal simplicity of the prose, rendered in translation by Ellen Jones, highlights the brutality of the world created on these pages." — *3:AM Magazine*

"An atmospheric, expansive story of melancholy situated somewhere between the Pacific Ocean and the Atacama Desert… *Nancy* works at the height of fiction's power to bring us closer to others." — *ArtsHub* (5/5 stars)

"[*Nancy*] uncovers the painful wounds inflicted by belief and by poverty, when life has become a wilderness, a minefield, an act of survival, in which even love and desire are reduced to nothing, witnesses to a happiness as improbable as it is precarious." — Leonardo Sanhueza

"We have here an extremely sensitive, intelligent, talented writer… A marvel." — Rodrigo Hidalgo, *El Guillatún*

NANCY

BRUNO LLORET

Translated from Spanish by
ELLEN JONES

TWO LINES
PRESS

First published in Chile as *Nancy* by Editorial Cuneta, 2015

Copyright © 2015 by Bruno Lloret

C/O Puentes Agency

Translation copyright © 2020 by Ellen Jones

English translation first published in Australia by Giramondo Publishing, 2020

Cover design by Gabriele Wilson

Cover photo by Heike Bors / Millennium Images, UK

Design by Sloane | Samuel

Printed in Canada

Two Lines Press

582 Market Street, Suite 700, San Francisco, CA 94104

www.twolinespress.com

ISBN: 978-1-949641-12-7

Ebook ISBN: 978-1-949641-13-4

Library of Congress Cataloging-in-Publication Data

Names: Lloret, Bruno, author. | Jones, Ellen, 1989– translator.
Title: Nancy / Bruno Lloret; translated from Spanish by Ellen Jones.
Other titles: Nancy. English
Description: San Francisco, CA: Two Lines Press, [2021] | Summary: "A
  dying woman relives her youth in this heartrending novel punctuated by
  graves, footprints, x-rays, and crosses"-- Provided by publisher.
Identifiers: LCCN 2020030574 (print) | LCCN 2020030575 (ebook)
ISBN 9781949641127 (hardcover) | ISBN 9781949641134 (ebook)
Classification: LCC PQ8098.422.L67 N3613 2021 (print)
LCC PQ8098.422.L67 (ebook) | DDC 863/.7--dc23
LC record available at https://lccn.loc.gov/2020030574
LC ebook record available at https://lccn.loc.gov/2020030575

1 3 5 7 9 10 8 6 4 2

This project is supported in part by an award from the National Endowment
for the Arts.

NATIONAL
ENDOWMENT for the ARTS
arts.gov

For Marina, Nova, and Samuel

The farther you walk from home,
the longer the way back.

— Mormon proverb

XXXXXXXXXXXXXXXXXXXXXXX
XXXXXXXXXXXXXXXXXXXXXXX
XXXXXXXXXXXXXXXXXXXXXXX
XXXXXXXXXXXXXXXXXXXXXXX
XXXXXXXXXXXXXXXXXXXXXXX
XXXXXXXXXXXXXXXXXXXXXXX
XXXXXXXXXXXXXXXXXXXXXXX
XXXXXXXXXXXXXXXXXXXXXXX
XXXXXXXXXXXXXXXXXXXXXXX
XXXXXXXXXXXXXXXXXXXXXXX
XXXXXXXXXXXXXXXXXXXXXXX
XXXXXXXXXXXXXXXXXXXXXXX
XXXXXXXXXXXXXXXXXXXXXXX
XXXXXXXXXXXXXXXXXXXXXXX
XXXXXXXXXXXXXXXXXXXXXXX
XXXXXXXXXXXXXXXXXXXXXXX
XXXXXXXXXXXXXXXXXXXXXXX
XXXXXXXXXXXXXXXXXXXXXXX
XXXXXXXXXXXXXXXXXXXXXXX
XXXXXXXXXXXXXXXXXXXXXXX
XXXXXXXXXXXXXXXXXXXXXXX
XXXXXXXXXXXXXXXXXXXXXXX
XXXXXXXXXXXXXXXXXXXXXXX
XXXXXXXXXXXXXXXXXXXXXXX
XXXXXXXXXXXXXXXXXXXXXXX
XXXXXXXXXXXXXXXXXXXXXXX
XXXXXXXXXXXXXXXXXXXXXXX
XXXXXXXXXXXXXXXXXXXXXXX
XXXXXXXXXXXXXXXXXXXXXXX
XXXXXXXXXXXXXXXXXXXXXXX

✘✘✘✘✘✘✘✘✘✘✘✘✘✘✘✘✘✘✘✘✘✘✘
✘✘✘✘✘✘✘✘✘✘✘✘✘✘✘✘✘✘✘✘✘✘✘
✘✘✘✘✘✘✘✘✘✘✘✘✘✘✘✘✘✘✘✘✘✘✘
✘✘✘✘✘✘✘✘✘✘✘✘✘✘✘✘✘✘✘✘✘✘✘
✘✘✘✘✘✘✘✘✘✘✘✘✘✘✘✘✘✘✘✘✘✘✘
✘✘✘✘✘✘✘✘✘✘✘✘✘✘✘✘✘✘✘✘✘✘✘
✘✘✘✘✘✘✘✘✘✘✘✘✘✘✘✘✘✘✘✘✘✘✘
✘✘✘✘✘✘✘✘✘✘✘✘✘✘✘✘✘✘✘✘✘✘✘
✘✘✘✘✘✘✘✘✘✘✘✘✘✘✘✘✘✘✘✘✘✘✘
✘✘✘✘✘✘✘✘✘✘✘✘✘✘✘✘✘✘✘✘✘✘✘
✘✘✘✘✘✘✘✘✘✘✘✘✘✘✘✘✘✘✘✘✘✘✘
✘✘✘✘✘✘✘✘✘✘✘✘✘✘✘✘✘✘✘✘✘✘✘
✘✘✘✘✘✘✘✘✘✘✘✘✘✘✘✘✘

And one morning the horn sounded ✘ ✘ ✘ ✘ ✘
My eyes snapped open ✘ ✘ I rolled over and looked
at his face, that moustache of his longer than ever,
those broomstick eyebrows ✘ ✘ A perfect mask of
loneliness ✘ I gave him a long hug, and just said
                    they've come for me
                    see you
      ✘   ✘   ✘   ✘

            ✘ Papá santo, my saintly father, heaved a
sigh and turned his face to the wall. I took my
things and left ✘   ✘   ✘

         ✘✘✘✘✘ And so it went ✘✘✘✘✘

   ✘   ✘   The convoy was much bigger this time ✘
✘ ✘ ✘ ✘ At least ten trucks ✘✘ The dogs from
the salt mine, hanging around the entrance to the

warehouse where we'd been sleeping, watched them warily, uneasy at the growl of the engines ✖ ✖ ✖ ✖ ✖ ✖A growl that thickened the atmosphere ✖ ✖ ✖
✖ And the sun rising over the gorges ✖
✖ The white of the sky watching over us

✖ ✖ Get a move on, chilena, said Jesulé ✖ ✖ ✖
✖ You going to Bolivia?
✖ Course. Told you, didn't I: this is the last run we're doing ✖ ✖
✖ ✖ Where in Bolivia though? ✖ ✖
✖ ✖ Figure it out when we get there. See what the deal is, he replied. Wherever we can get the best price for the cars ✖ ✖ ✖ ✖ ✖
✖ I asked him for a smoke, pretended to inhale, and said:
I already gave you all my money. More than two hundred lucas. I gotta get out of here ✖ ✖
✖ Easy now, he replied, that's why we're here. I told you we weren't gonna ditch you. Plus we'll be quick, you'll be home in an hour ✖ ✖ ✖
✖ No, I don't wanna go home✖ ✖
✖ ✖ ✖ ✖ ✖ ✖ ✖ ✖ ✖ ✖ ✖ ✖
✖ ✖ ✖ Where d'you wanna go then? ✖ ✖ ✖
✖ Bolivia, with you guys ✖ ✖ ✖
✖ ✖ ✖ ✖ ✖ ✖ ✖ And how am I sposed to get you through, paisa? he said, dismissing the plan with a wave of his hand ✖ ✖ ✖ ✖ ✖ ✖ ✖
✖ That's your problem, I answered, dead serious ✖ ✖ ✖ ✖

✕ ✕ ✕ ✕ ✕ ✕ ✕ ✕ ✕ ✕ ✕ ✕ ✕ ✕ ✕ ✕ ✕
✕ ✕ ✕ ✕ ✕ ✕ ✕ ✕ ✕ ✕ ✕ ✕ ✕ ✕ ✕ ✕ ✕
✕ ✕ ✕ ✕ It was all I needed to say ✕ ✕ ✕
They put me under a tarp with a bunch of metal poles and pegs, rolled up inside a tent ✕ ✕ ✕ I had water, bread, mortadella ✕ ✕ And I spent thirteen hours in the dark, choking on dust, completely numb ✕ ✕ ✕ When they let me out to stretch my bones I'd already pissed myself twice ✕ ✕ ✕ ✕ ✕ I slept in snatches full of sad dreams ✕ ✕ ✕

✕ the kind you never remember after you wake up, but still, when you open your eyes there's a real ache in your chest ✕

✕ ✕ ✕ ✕ ✕ ✕ ✕ ✕ The third time I got out for a breather they said we were past Oruro, so I could sit shotgun ✕ ✕ ✕ ✕ ✕ ✕ ✕ ✕

✕ I couldn't stop staring at the landscape, dazed by the light and open space ✕ ✕ ✕ ✕ ✕ ✕ ✕ ✕ ✕ ✕ ✕ ✕ ✕

✕ ✕ The sky was a transparent ceiling three meters above my head ✕ ✕ ✕ ✕ ✕ ✕

✕ Right: Where do you want us to drop you, kid? Jesulé asked ✕ ✕ ✕ Three Romany guys were watching, leaning against the only truck still with us ✕ ✕ ✕ ✕ ✕ ✕

✕ The rest of the convoy had disappeared some-where along the main road ✕ ✕ ✕ From the base of the mountain a tangle of sheep streamed toward us ✖ ✖ ✖ A couple of dogs nipping here and there to keep the flow on course ✖ ✖ ✖ ✖ Behind them, a Bolivian with hard cracked skin, like coal ✖ ✖ ✖

✖ ✖ When that guy gets here I'll tell you where I want you to leave me ✖ ✖ ✖ ✖ ✖ ✖ ✖

✖ ✖ We sat on a sharp rock ✖ ✖ ✖ ✖ ✖ Jesulé was trying to stay stony-faced, pretending to be pissed off ✖ ✖ Three sheep stopped to lick the salt off my fingers, and I let them, cracking up, happy ✖ ✖ The shepherd tipped his hat as he passed us ✖ ✖ ✖ Jesulé asked him about the weather ✖ ✖

✖ The old man looked at the sky, at the mountains apparently holding it up, and said: All good, it's going to be clear ✖ ✖ ✖ ✖

✖He asked for a cigarette and sat down to smoke ✖✖✖✖

✖With every drag he came back to life a bit more, his eyes brightening ✖ ✖ ✖ ✖ ✖ ✖ He smiled and offered us some coca in thanks ✖ ✖ ✖ ✖ ✖ ✖ ✖ ✖ ✖ ✖ ✖ ✖ ✖ ✖ ✖ ✖ ✖ ✖ While I was making a ball of leaves with my tongue I asked him how he was so sure it would be clear ✖ ✖ ✖ Because of the clouds, he said ✖ ✖ ✖ ✖ ✖ ✖ Look at them and you'll know if things'll turn out right ✖ So what are they saying now? I asked ✖ ✖ ✖ ✖ Nothing, señorita. Can't you see there aren't any? ✖ ✖ ✖ ✖ ✖ ✖ ✖ ✖ ✖ ✖ ✖ ✖ ✖ ✖ ✖ ✖

✖ I bowed my head and concentrated on throwing rocks at rocks ✖ ✖ I looked at the mountain, the foothills, the sheep: in the wake of the flock there wasn't a single plant left ✗ And how d'you know when something bad's gonna happen? ✗ He hushed the dogs with his hand and sent them back to keep the flock in check. As he waved goodbye, he said: Just look at the shadows of the clouds on the mountains ✗ Clouds are good news ✗ Their shadows are bad news ✗ It's all the same thing ✗

✖ ✖ ✖ ✖ ✖ ✖ ✖ ✖ ✖ ✖ ✖ ✖ ✖ ✖ ✖ ✖ ✖
✖ ✖ ✖ ✖ ✖ ✖ ✖ ✖ ✖ ✖ ✖ ✖ ✖ ✖ ✖ ✖ ✖
✖ ✖ ✖ ✖ ✖ ✖ ✖ ✖ ✖ ✖ ✖ ✖ ✖ ✖ ✖ ✖ ✖
✖ ✖ ✖ ✖ ✖ ✖ ✖ ✖
✖ ✖ ✖ ✖ ✖ ✖ ✖ ✖ ✖ ✖ ✖ ✖ ✖

✖ ✖ Santa Cruz, I told Jesulé as he maneuvered us back onto the main road. Take me to Santa Cruz. The Romany nodded ✖ ✖ We were quiet for a couple of hours ✖ ✖ ✖ ✖✖ ✖✖

✖ What'd ya lose there? ✖ ✖ ✖ ✖ ✖ ✖ ✖ ✖ ✖ ✖ ✖ ✖

✖ Nothing. I am trying to lose a Romany though, I answered ✖

Your old man beat you so hard you had to come all the way out here? ✖ ✖ ✖ ✖ ✖ ✖ ✖ ✖ ✖ ✖ ✖ ✖ ✖ ✖ ✖ ✖ ✖ ✖ ✖ I ignored him ✖ ✖ ✖ ✖ ✖ ✖ ✖ ✖ ✖ ✖ ✖ ✖ ✖ ✖ ✖ ✖ I was concentrating on the clouds, the absence of clouds, their shadows, the mountains ✖

✖ ✖ ✖ ✖ ✖

When we were still a couple of hours away I managed to fall asleep, my face trembling against the glass ✖ ✖ ✖ ✖ ✖ It's important to rest your bones ✖ Your brain ✖ ✖ ✖ ✖ ✖ ✖ ✖ ✖ ✖ ✖ ✖ I also started dreaming again. I dreamed of an abandoned valley, full of rabbits and hawthorn, overseen by five dogs ✖ ✖ ✖ ✖ ✖ At the end of a path a giant mestizo kid was wiggling his toes beside an abandoned adobe church ✖ ✖ ✖ The roof was sagging ✖ Between the mestizo kid's huge legs there were three graves ✖ ✖ ✖ The first was unrecognizable ✖ Barely a pile of stones. The second had its inscription worn away. The third was fresh, a recent grave ✖ ✖ ✖ ✖ ✖ ✖ ✖ ✖ ✖ The child was enormous: the bell tower came up to his knees and his belly button was out of sight above the clouds. When he laughed, sky and earth connected in a crackle of violet lightning ✖ ✖ ✖ Shadows writhed on the ground ✖ ✖ In the dream he laughed so long and loud his laugh became a wail ✖ ✖

✖ ✖ I woke up to Jesulé shaking me ✖ ✖ ✖ The truck was on the outskirts of a city. We were waiting at a red light in front of a square unlike any I'd seen before ✖ Surrounded by arched colonnades and streets lined with palm trees ✖ ✖ ✖ ✖ First thing I noticed was the humidity. The place was suffocating ✖

✖ ✖ ✖ ✖ ✖ ✖ ✖ ✖ Are we there?

✖ ✖ ✖ ✖ ✖ ✖ ✖ ✖ ✖ ✖ ✖ We're here, he replied, lighting one cigarette with the butt of another, obviously pissed off. Get changed and get out, kid. This is you ✖

✖ Someone honked impatiently and Jesulé put his foot down, but we didn't get far: he had to brake suddenly to avoid running over a stooped old gringo hidden under a blue cap, bags under his eyes, his beard damp with midday hunger ✖   ✖

Whoredom and wine and new wine
take away the heart.
Hosea 4:11

✗ ✗   As soon as I set foot on the streets of Santa Cruz I felt like the world was going to split apart where I stood ✗ ✗ ✗   I tried to look at the clouds and figure out how to read them, while thinking about what I could sell from my backpack to get some money. But the clouds, even when there weren't any, were different than the ones in Oruro ✗ ✗ ✗ ✗ ✗ ✗ Or maybe we chilenos can only read them on the mountains ✗ ✗ ✗ ✗ ✗ ✗ ✗ ✗ Their sunset colors ✗ ✗ Black, blue, flamingo pink ✗ ✗ Something stays with you after all that time ✗ ✗ Like having a family member always within sight ✗ That's what I was thinking ✗ ✗ ✗ ✗ ✗ ✗ I stopped looking at the sky after that ✗ ✗ ✗ ✗ ✗ ✗

   ✗ Sitting on a bench in the corner of the square, I saw him again, walking over from the other side

✖✖✖ He looked confused ✖ ✖ ✖ Going in circles, weaving around people, for a good twenty minutes ✖ ✖ Sometimes he'd get close and sneak a look at me ✖✖✖✖✖✖ I caught on quick and stared back, serious, then out of nowhere he untensed his shoulders and came right over, no weaving this time ✖✖✖   ✖✖✖   ✖✖✖   ✖✖✖   ✖✖✖ ✖✖✖   ✖✖✖   ✖✖✖ He said: I know you. You used to live in Ch, near the big port. Isn't your name Carla? I told him he was right except for the name, recognizing the same roughness in his accent as those gringos we used to go to Playa Roja with sometimes ✖ ✖ ✖

✖ ✖ ✖ My name's Nancy ✖ ✖ ✖   ✖ ✖ ✖ ✖ ✖ ✖ He smiled and asked me out for a bite to eat ✖ ✖ ✖ ✖ ✖ ✖ ✖ When I saw him up close I realized he was the same lost gringo we'd almost run over just now ✖ ✖ ✖ ✖ We shook hands clumsily and headed to a Chicken Palace ✖ ✖ ✖ ✖ There he asked me to marry him before I'd eaten a single fry ✖ ✖ ✖ ✖ I looked at him for a second, terrified he wouldn't let me eat if I said no ✖ ✖ ✖ ✖ ✖ ✖ ✖ I shoved a couple of fries in my mouth and, as they turned to mash between my teeth, I considered him carefully ✖ ✖ ✖ ✖ Judging by his looks, I reckon Tim couldn't have been more than thirty-five at the time. I was seventeen ✖ ✖ ✖ ✖ ✖ I said yes then and there and we went to live in Guayaquil, until one day we realized, out walking in a tropical rainstorm, that we didn't belong there but in Chile ✖ ✖ ✖ We decided to move back and settle in this disgusting port town, where rum and Teletrak betting took my husband from me ✖ Over twenty years Tim managed to lose every job imaginable, till no one except the Japanese would hire him ✖ Working for the Japanese was a kind of slow death sentence ✖ He'd leave one day and spend two weeks offshore with two hundred other hired hands, trawling and processing and canning the fish right there on the boat ✖ He always came back smiling, serene, but it didn't last. He'd go straight to some bar and spend the night getting loaded with his friends

✖ Still, we were fond of each other, even after we grew apart ✖ While I waited for him I'd remember nights when I'd stare at the sky for hours on end, lying on the barren earth outside the vacant lot by my house in Ch. I felt closer to everything I saw up there than I did to that idiot ✖

Booze got the better of him. Every night. Without fail. ✖ ✖ ✖

✖ ✖ ✖

And I'd think: When did you agree to this, Nancy? ✖ ✖ ✖ ✖ ✖ When did you agree to live like a widow before your time?
✖ ✖ ✖ ✖   ✖ ✖

It was Tim that got me listening to the radio, to stop from feeling lonely and because I was tired of talking to myself ✖

I'd say aloud to myself: It's like I'm his damn mother

✖   He worried me so much. I'd imagine him dead somewhere, even though Tim was a lucky old drunk: he never did get hurt and would always show up eventually, when everything had finally shut, out cold, dragged home by some loser. Once he was stretched out on the sofa he'd be there for hours, that gringo of mine. Eventually he'd get up, shower, go and buy some hake and vegetables and make me the best dinner in the world. I'd watch him and worry just as much as I did when he wasn't there, my chest hurting like he'd never come home at all ✖ We'd eat in silence, hardly speaking, and then we'd make love in the dark for five minutes, on a good day ✖ The last time we did it was the day I told Tim I was dying of cancer. We stared at each other like divers underwater, sunk in uncertainty, until I poured another glass of wine to break the silence ✖ Then he took me by the hand and led me to bed, like when we did it in Santa Cruz all that time ago, the first time, and while he took off his pants I lay down on my stomach and waited, burning, dying, but happy, for him to give it to me ✖ Instead of crying I held in the need to pee and crushed my face into a pillow ✖ Tim was so rough it felt like the handful of times I'd slept with Jesulé ✖ ✖ ✖ While he was doing it he asked me: Are you sure? I said, Of course, the doctor told me it was a miracle I was still alive, really. He gave a couple more thrusts and, coming inside me, let out an electric moan, horrible, like he was in pain ✖ I needed to piss so badly a couple of drops actually came out ✖ I ran to the bathroom and pissed for three whole minutes, nonstop. Through the door I could see the silhouette of my husband, lying on the bed, panting, and I felt an oppressive heat rise up through my legs from the freezing tiles ✖ I pressed the soles of my feet onto the floor and then lifted them up, transfixed by the sweaty prints they left on the white tiles, by the way they slowly disappeared, and I thought: Why can't cancer be like this, why can't it disappear, like words, like cigarettes

```
        ✖       ✖       ✖       ✖
        ✖✖      ✖       ✖       ✖               ✖✖
✖       ✖       ✖       ✖       ✖               ✖✖
✖       ✖       ✖       ✖       ✖               ✖✖
   ✖    ✖       ✖       ✖       ✖               ✖✖
✖       ✖       ✖               ✖               ✖✖
✖       ✖       ✖       ✖       ✖               ✖✖
✖       ✖✖      ✖       ✖       ✖               ✖✖
✖       ✖       ✖       ✖       ✖               ✖✖
✖✖      ✖       ✖       ✖       ✖               ✖✖
✖       ✖       ✖       ✖       ✖               ✖✖
✖       ✖       ✖       ✖       ✖               ✖✖
✖       ✖               ✖       ✖               ✖
✖       ✖       ✖               ✖                   ✖
✖       ✖✖      ✖       ✖       ✖               ✖✖
   ✖    ✖       ✖       ✖       ✖               ✖
✖       ✖       ✖       ✖       ✖               ✖✖
✖       ✖✖      ✖       ✖       ✖               ✖
✖       ✖       ✖       ✖       ✖               ✖✖
```

✕✕　✕　　✕　　　✕　　✕　　　✕✕
✕　　✕　　　　　　✕　　✕　　　✕✕
✕　　✕　　✕　　✕　　✕　　　　✕
✕✕　✕　　✕　　✕　　✕　　　✕✕
✕　　✕　　✕　　　　　✕　　　✕✕
✕　　✕　　　　　✕　　✕　　　✕✕
✕✕　✕　　✕　　✕　　✕　　　✕✕
✕　　✕　　✕　　✕　　✕　　　　✕
✕✕　✕　　　　　✕　　✕　　　✕✕
✕　　✕　　✕　　✕　　✕　　　✕✕
✕　　✕　　✕　　✕　　✕　　　✕✕
✕✕　✕　　✕　　✕　　✕　　　　✕
✕　　✕　　　　　✕　　✕　　　✕✕
✕　　✕　　✕　　✕　　✕　　　✕✕
✕　　✕　　✕　　✕　　✕　　　✕
✕　　✕　　✕　　✕　　✕　　　✕✕
✕　　✕　　✕　　✕　　✕　　　　✕
✕　　✕　　✕　　✕　　✕　　　✕✕

One day the young doctor, the latest doctor to check over my x-rays, asked me: Have you looked at them, doña Nancy? I said, Yes, every day in the bathroom, held up to the light. And I thought about saying: Have you noticed the shapes that reveal themselves when we look at an x-ray?

Some are like deepwater fish
(Have you ever been deep underwater?)

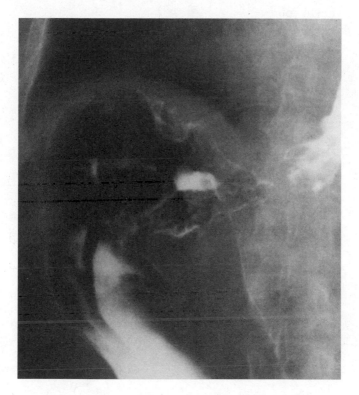

1032C

In others there are ghosts
(Of the lepers Jesus cured in those Semana Santa films, for example)
(Have you ever seen a ghost?)

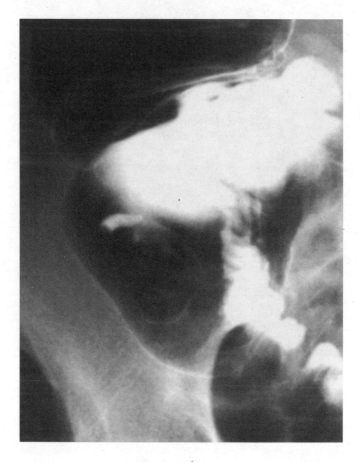

1222b

Butterflies, a monstrous imbunche, three masks emerging from the abyss

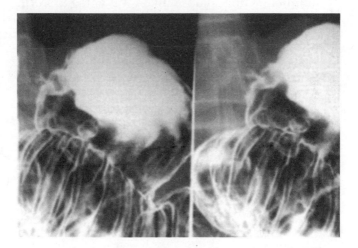

1474a

Well what do you want me to say, then, Nancy? the doctor asked, fiddling with his wedding ring and checking the clock on the table. If you already know them by heart we may as well call it a day. Please fill out the form before you go ✖ Alright, doc, it's not like I'm dying or anything, I said as I took the morphine prescription, acting all upset like I was going to storm off. But turns out that was exactly what the doctor wanted. He said nothing, didn't even move. So for the sake of pride I had to keep pretending to be offended and retreat, holding the papers and x-rays like a shield.

✖ ✖ ✖

✖ ✖ ✖

For the next three months neither of us mentioned it. When I saw Tim for the first time after they removed my breasts and uterus, when he got back from trawling, his face remained serene ✖ He asked me to show him ✖ Embarrassed, I took off my dressing gown and we looked at me together: where my breasts and belly button used to be it was like I'd been zipped up ✖ The morning light came through the window and I felt completely alone ✖ Tim said: Like an Amazon. That was all. He hugged me, carefully, made a quick lunch, then went out drinking ✖ When he was upset, his nose, red and broken, used to twitch up and down ✖ His eyes, slanted and blue, used to glisten a bit under his cap, though you'd never notice unless you knew him really well ✖ He'd breathe through his mouth and moisten his lips ✖

Those were the signs ✖

He looked unfazed but I knew he needed a drink.
Knew I wouldn't see him for a good while ✖
✖✖✖✖✖✖✖✖✖✖✖✖✖✖✖✖✖✖✖✖✖✖
✖✖✖   ✖ ✖ ✖ ✖ ✖ ✖ ✖
✖ ✖ ✖ ✖ ✖ ✖ ✖ ✖ ✖ ✖ ✖ ✖ ✖

The chemotherapy was looming and I decided to
shave my head so I didn't have to see my hair fall out
in big handfuls ✖ I did it alone, so when Tim came
back from his stint offshore and found me pale and
shivering, my skull wrapped in a multicolored scarf,
the only thing he could think to do was give me a kiss
on the forehead then go back to his same old shit ✖
He left, dragging his feet.

And that was that.

✖

✖

✖

Knowing you're going to die is horrible not just
because you don't want to die, but also because there's
always some residual, surviving doubt. It survived in
me alright, a fledgling hope, hiding behind the eyes.
Even though I was skeletal, mutilated, barren ✖

✖ I thought: No motherfucker should have to
die alone like this ✖ ✖ ✖

If only the world had ended in 2012 like everyone
said it would, that would have been perfect ✖ ✖ ✖
✖ ✖ ✖ ✖ ✖ ✖ ✖   I was twelve that year—I
had Pato, and my mamá wasn't so crazy, or at least
I felt I could handle her ✖ ✖ ✖ ✖ ✖ And now?
What have you got left, Nancy? ✖ ✖ ✖ ✖ ✖ ✖ ✖
Hope? ✖ ✖ ✖ ✖

Sometimes when I woke up, even if I was really tired, it didn't feel like I was dying. How could I be, when there was still a body reflected in the mirror ✖ ✖ ✖ ✖ ✖

✖ But the locals took it upon themselves to remind me · ✖   ✖   In the street, people simply stopped saying hello, and this drove me to complete despair. Weeks could go by when the only reason I didn't talk to myself was because the radio was on at full volume, and then only because I couldn't hear my own voice ✖

Under my breath, I'd whisper the names of musicians:
Chavela Vargas, pray for us
Palmenia Pizarro, thy kingdom come
Orquesta Huambalí, thy will be done, on earth as it is…

✖ After a while, that silence is worse than being at death's door ✖ Maybe even worse than hope ✖
✖
✖

The side effects of chemotherapy eventually kicked in, and I went into a slow decline: I barely ate, and spent long hours in bed, lying half-asleep, feeling all the bones in my body tightening ✖ ✖ ✖ In rare hours of lucidity I'd try half-heartedly to shower or wash up. The water was so cold, like metal, even when it was boiling, so instead I had to sit shivering on the toilet and wipe my entire body clean with a cloth ✖ ✖ In the kitchen I'd rinse the dirty plates and cutlery under the tap, struggling to hold them by the edges to avoid the chills I got from touching the water ✖ ✖ ✖

✖ I devoted myself to contemplating the dust invasion. I couldn't really believe it. I sort of thought that if I looked at it long enough the dirt might somehow disappear ✖

It didn't ✖

And the pain
and the mannequins in the street
old ladies with waxen skin
and me turning to papier-mâché

✖ Don't even get me started on the NAUSEA ✖

A couple of days before I started taking morphine—I may as well have had no husband by this point, the gringo wasn't even coming home to sleep anymore—a friend of Tim's banged on the door, waited the fifteen minutes it took me to get out of bed and drag myself out front, and said, quickly, not looking me in the eye, that my husband had been involved in an accident offshore and had gone to a better place ✖   ✖   ✖
✖   ✖ What happened? I asked ✖ ✖   ✖   ✖
✖   ✖ He was sucked into the tuna processor ✖
✖   ✖   ✖ And his body? ✖ ✖   ✖   ✖
✖   ✖   ✖   ✖   There is no body, he replied, and, after he'd hugged me, added that some-one would come on behalf of the Japanese to give

me their condolences and a check for the funeral ✖
And that was that: an hour later an official—short,
barely comprehensible, bowing continually—told me
he was sorry for my loss, and that they'd cover all
the expenses, the funeral and that sort of thing, but
unfortunately they couldn't give me any compensa-
tion because, according to the insurance company's
medical examination, Tim had been drunk when the
accident happened ✖ As I listened to this diminutive
Japanese specimen I leaned against the doorframe,
trying not to pass out from pain, and struggled to
understand what the fuck was going on ✖ I shook
my head and asked again about his body ✖   ✖
The Japanese man looked displeased, like it was
rude to demand to see the gringo's remains after
he'd explained what had happened, and although in
the end he said nothing I imagined him replying,
coolly, that the only thing he could do was give me
a moment alone with the 2,500 cans containing my
deceased husband ✖

✖ (In fact, I'm convinced he was perfectly capable of
saying it, only he rushed off after giving me the check
so as not to waste any more time) ✖ ✖

That afternoon I took out my grandmother's First
Communion dress and dyed it with aniline. While
it was hanging in the sun, dripping black water, I
polished my shoes and stood in front of the mirror,
preparing myself for the wake, which would be the
next day in the fishermen's chapel. All night I lay on

the bed in my widow's clothes, eyes open, waiting till it was time

✖ A few workers from the processing plant came to the chapel, mainly women, but that was it really ✖ The burial was even emptier ✖ After the final shovelful of earth, the last few stragglers dispersed silently, not daring to give their condolences, and I went back to being a ghost ✖ The only person who continued to give me the time of day during this whole nightmare was Isidorita. A kindly fat woman who comes and looks after me every now and then ✖ ✖ ✖ ✖ ✖ ✖ ✖ We share our regrets sometimes, quietly, and I try to console her ✖ ✖ ✖ ✖ ✖ ✖ ✖ ✖ ✖ ✖ ✖ ✖ ✖ ✖ ✖ ✖ ✖ ✖ She'd wanted to be the carnival queen and everyone had laughed at her ✖ ✖ ✖ ✖ ✖ ✖ When we ran into each other in the street she looked like a kindred spirit. She saw me sunk in a void, alone. I saw how anxious she was, everyone acting all friendly then laughing behind her back ✖ ✖ ✖ ✖ ✖ ✖ ✖ ✖ ✖ Sometimes they laughed in her face, too ✖ ✖ ✖ ✖ ✖ I love that she talks to me, that she washes the dishes, and most of all that she tries to smile between sighs ✖ ✖ ✖ ✖ ✖ ✖ She convinces me, more easily each time, to turn on the TV so we don't miss *Sparrowhawks of Christ*: Juan the missionary under the jungle palms, exchanging glances with Enriqueta ✖ ✖ ✖ Sweating as they clean the lepers' wounds, hearts racing, completely smitten with each other ✖ ✖ ✖

The morphine means I'm usually sunk in a dream even more painful than the cancer eating away at my bones ✖ When the gringo was alive I at least had someone to worry about, but it all went SO fast

Here I am, waiting.

Honor thy father and thy mother, as the Lord thy God hath
commanded thee; that thy days may be prolonged, and that
it may go well with thee, in the land which the Lord thy
God giveth thee.
Deuteronomy 5:16

When I was little my mamá threatened to sell us to
the Romany. She'd point at us, at me and Pato, and
say that all we did was bring the family bad luck and
unnecessary expense ✖ She'd walk around in circles,
twitching the curtains, rearranging her collection
of figurines on the shelf, and, when she was tired,
she'd sit at the table with that ridiculous little box
between her fingers: Our Daily Bread. Before every
meal, or when there was something to discuss, or
really whenever the woman felt like it, she'd pull a
Bible verse from the box to reflect on, to hold on to
while the storm lasted ✖ ✖ She used to read them
out so furiously that I felt like I was facing a tribunal,
listening to a secret verdict, a verdict that would have
horrible consequences ✖

✖ My papá would just keep reading, if he was reading, or scratching his forearm and drinking soda,

wiping his brow with a handkerchief ✖ His patience and silence were ways of enduring the wife he had chosen to build a home for him

Ways of escaping inside himself

✖ But we didn't fit inside my papá, however big he might be, so my brother and I, shooting each other terrified glances, anticipating a smack around the head, would run out into the courtyard whenever we could, hoping to be left in peace for the afternoon. Outside I'd cry, snot-nosed, my back against the brick, while Pato patiently built a tower out of boxes ✖ We'd stand, leaning on the top of the wall, looking out at the scrubby patch of land behind the house, letting ourselves be loved by the winter sun, watching the minutes go by, mourning the calm that had been lost and praying it would hurry up and return ✖ Shouts sounded inside. Just two or three. Sharp and stifled. When we saw the door handle move my brother would balance on the top of the wall and help me climb over to the vacant lot beyond ✖ Before he jumped down with me he'd kick away the boxes ✖ Mamá would let out a couple of shrieks, sticking her head out into the courtyard, promising to give us a thrashing as soon as we came back ✖ Sitting in the shadow of the wall, our legs stretched out in front of us, all we could think to do was to stay out until after our parents had fallen asleep.

During those long hours, while the sun was going down, I'd ask Pato if he thought they were really going to sell us to the Romany. He'd look at me, serious, and shake his head:

Don't ask stupid questions ✖ ✖
Little sisters don't ask stupid questions ✖ ✖ ✖ ✖
✖ ✖ ✖ ✖ ✖ ✖ ✖ ✖ ✖ ✖

And he'd fall silent, his face as hard as he could make it

✖ After a while I'd get up and walk down to the sea ✖ Just before I stepped from soil to sand, where the beach supposedly began, my older brother would yell down to me ✖ And I'd wait for him ✖

With the wind roaring in my ears, my feet sinking into the sand, I'd relax a bit and stop crying. I'd rest my head on his arm and he'd laugh at me for throwing a tantrum worthy of La Chilindrina, that kid from the Mexican TV show, and we'd comment on the scenery to be found along the beach:

bitches and their pups, empty bottles, old truck tires, debris, dry grass,

ice cream wrappers, textbooks, beer cans, spray paints, disoriented guinea pigs.

Further back, abandoned houses, graffiti, a couple of flocks of evangelicals, all of them wearing straw hats and suits that smelled of soap, walking through the streets of Ch like they were crossing the desert.[1]

✖ ✖

When it was time to leave, Pato scaled the wall in a single leap. I listened, attentive to what was happening on the other side of the bricks. I heard him building the staircase out of boxes again. It worried me that he might never reappear, but always, after the usual noises, he'd stick his face over the top, smiling, and pull me over in one go, back into the courtyard ✖ Then we'd climb the stairs with our shoes in our hands, holding our breath, and once we were in the bedroom we'd talk quietly, lying on the same bed, until we fell asleep.

✖ ✖
✖

---

[1] "The desert of the spirit is in the heart of every city, Sister Nancy," I heard the bible-bashers say a while back, on the playground, when I was still a worthy interlocutor, when I was something to be envied even, when some people thought the only reason we didn't preach or pray was because the head of my family was some sort of occult pastor. "Come to the town square with us one day and see the way they look at us, the people who are listening. They way they pity us. Then look at how we look at the people looking at us. The way we pity them." The sad thing, I always thought, was that nobody was listening, everyone was looking, even though the Gospel was a kind of soundtrack.

All this had been going on more or less forever and it gave me dreadful nightmares ✖ Every time I saw a group of Romany in the street, sitting in the square or spread out along the high streets, offering their palm readings and aura cleansings; every time I went with my papá in the car to the big port and saw the men sitting at the crossroads, a pair of tents on the pavement half-bleached by sun and the passage of time, encouraging passengers to buy the copper pans on display; every time they came up to the car and I smelled their sour smell, a mix of sweat and grime, I'd want to die ✖   One frequent nightmare was that at night the house was invaded by these golden witches, their breasts hanging under their dresses and their underarms full of hair. With claws that were sharp and covered in rings they'd drag me by my feet and take me to live in their camp ✖   Sometimes, in the nightmare, I ended up begging with the rest of the scrawny children who'd been kidnapped and dragged the length of Chile from south to north, fleeing the winter. In others they locked me in a cage and whenever they could, they'd make me dance in the markets to the rhythm of the saddest music, dressed in next to nothing, my neck bound in an iron shackle that heated up as I moved my feet over the sand ✖ And so it went: just when I couldn't move my legs any faster, when the faces of the old Romany women were melding into the smoke of the cigarettes they puffed continually; just when the little drum played by one of my fellow slave girls was giving out, I'd wake up screaming, my hands pressing down on my bladder. I'd open my eyes, see that everything was dark, lie back on the pillow, and feel a powerful, endless stream, flowing and flowing, soaking everything ✖ ✖ ✖ ✖ ✖

My brother would run and get some towels to try and clear up the mess, but it was no use. The old woman snapped awake at my screaming, and we'd hear her hotfooting it down the corridor in her flip-flops (like this: slap, slap, slap). We'd be shitting ourselves because she always beat the hell out of the both of us ✖

First she'd make me sit on the edge of the bed and watch my brother's bum turn into a cherry, while he looked straight ahead without moving a muscle. His face was a mask. When mamá got tired, Pato would pull up his pants and stand tall, as still as ever, until my turn was over and we found ourselves alone once again ✖ And together we'd coordinate our breathing, and it felt like when you're swimming and you catch a wave and rise up with it to the sky ✖ ✖ ✖

My brother was a superhero.

✖ ✖ The next morning I had to wash my mattress out on the patio while mamá peeled broad beans

and smoked, and took all her frustrations out on me.[2]
Later I had to go with my papá to the market in complete silence, my belly burning with shame ✖ ✖ ✖

    ✖ The calm would last until after lunch, or
thereabouts: then no matter what, for some reason
or other, she'd lose it with me again, and the threat
of the Romany became so real that despite Pato's
promises I felt like that same night they would be
coming for me. The rest of the day was black, and
the nightmare would return as soon as I drifted off,
and I'd piss myself once again ✖

✖ ✖ ✖ ✖ So that was every weekend and the odd
Tuesday or Wednesday too. The shame we shared,
me and my bladder.

(Saturdays and Sundays because those were the days
when there was booze in the house)

(Tuesdays and Wednesdays because those were the
days I went with my papá to La Gallineta, where all

---

[2] "Your dad's a queer. He's not the man I married. It's been
months since he touched me, and it's your fault. You can forget wearing any of the clothes in my wardrobe: it's staying
locked until you learn to be a woman. When you were born
I thought you were dead, and I wish I'd been right. I wish
the doctor'd wrung your tiny fucking neck. I wish you'd been
born dead dead dead. You fucked up my hips. Not even Pato
came out as big and ugly as you, you little bitch."

you had to do was sit at the bar, say hi, and wait for them to put the world's best hot dog down in front of you, a completo, the most complete completo, and half a liter of Coca-Cola)

✕ ✕ ✕ ✕ ✕ ✕   ✕ ✕ ✕ ✕ ✕
✕ ✕ ✕ ✕ ✕ ✕ ✕ ✕
✕ ✕ ✕ ✕ ✕ ✕ ✕ ✕ ✕ ✕ ✕ ✕ ✕
✕ ✕ ✕ ✕ ✕
✕ ✕ ✕ ✕ ✕ ✕ ✕ ✕ ✕

And then one day, a day like any other, it was my fourteenth birthday ✕ ✕ ✕ ✕
✕ ✕ ✕ ✕ ✕ ✕ ✕ ✕ ✕ ✕ ✕ ✕ ✕ ✕ ✕ ✕
✕ ✕ ✕ ✕ ✕ ✕ ✕ ✕ ✕ ✕ ✕ ✕

And the day of my birthday, Pato said: I'm going to look for work down in the big port. From then on I only saw him when he came to visit for the holidays ✕

There followed two years during which I had to learn to defend myself, to cultivate the art of not earning myself a smack for every little thing
✕ ✕ ✕ ✕ ✕ ✕ ✕ ✕ ✕ ✕ ✕ ✕ ✕ ✕ ✕ ✕ ✕ ✕

But before I knew it the summer arrived, and with it my brother. Everything seemed to acquire a calm that was impossible to achieve the rest of the year: he brought back muscles and stories, and in some sense the family came together around the life experiences of the first fledgling to leave the nest ✕ It lasted as long as it lasted ✖ That is: until Pato went missing outside a nightclub ✖

That same summer, as if I could forget, Sandra, who just over a month before had become my sister-in-law, got picked up for carrying a couple of twists of coke ✖ They locked her up, threw her in juvie in the big port ✖ Sandra was my classmate and she was lovely, lovely like nobody else. Ever since she was twelve she'd been going out dancing in bars and clubs with my brother and his friends, all at least five years older than her. She was a happy, active girl, restless and generous ✖ And Pato was simply the best man in the world, especially that period he was with Sandra. It was like they shined even brighter when they were together. I imagine, lying in this bed, what their lives would have been like somewhere else, if they'd had more luck, and it makes me so sad ✖ ✖ ✖

✖ ✖ ✖ But feeling sad won't change anything.
✖
✖
✖

Is there not an appointed time to man upon earth? Are not his days also like the days of an hireling? As a servant earnestly desireth the shadow, and as a hireling looketh for the reward of his work: So am I made to possess months of vanity, and wearisome nights are appointed to me. When I lie down, I say, When shall I arise, and the night be gone? And I am full of tossings to and fro unto the dawning of the day. My flesh is clothed with worms and clods of dust; my skin is broken, and become loathsome. My days are swifter than a weaver's shuttle, and are spent without hope.

Job 7:1–6

My father was a man with a lot to endure, a man who often seemed to be somewhere other than where he was ✖ Once a month mamá would go to the big port, supposedly to see Pato and her sister (a horrible creature, tall, cringing and decrepit, destroyed, gutted, gray) ✖ Because my father worked his body to the point of collapse, and when he wasn't working he was reading the Bible or watching TV, during those years I could, if I was quiet about it, go to the beaches north of town ✖ We were a crowd of twenty ✖ After lunch we'd walk along the coast, pissing ourselves laughing, till you could barely even see the houses in Ch

✖ The boys would run among the rocks, swim, collect sea urchins and starfish. They'd come and go

between the water and the beach. They'd stretch out on the sand, rolling over and over, till they looked like little strips of breaded flesh ✖   ✖   ✖
✖   ✖

✖ Us girls chatted by the water or swam out to where we could watch the boys. The older girls smoked and shared stories from nights out with real men ✖ We must have spent whole afternoons floating face up on the surface of the water or stretched out on the sand, talking about how guys our age were such idiots and how strong and good-looking they were once they'd done their military service ✖ ✖ ✖ ✖ ✖ ✖ In any case, those were moments of real happiness. The kinds of situations where you learn life's mysteries.

✖   ✖   One day, for example, Sandra peeled off from the group of girls floating in the water and disappeared ✖ When it was time to leave neither she nor Pato were anywhere to be seen ✖ One of the boys said they were fooling around down the beach, behind the rocks near the Quintrala cave ✖ I asked if they would go and look for them, but nobody moved ✖ I got up, furious, and walked between the big round rocks till I came across Pato's back shining in the sun. I went over all quiet and saw them up close: Sandra was sitting in front of him, cross-legged, sucking him off ✖ Contrary to expectation and despite my surprise, I found the image, then and still now, to be rather lovely. I thought: So that's how you suck someone off. How come it doesn't make her retch, the whole thing in her mouth like that. I answered my own question: I guess she's what Pato calls a sword-swallower ✖ I went over quietly until I was about two meters from them ✖ Sandra opened her eyes and, tilting her head, looked straight at me. Then she took the dick out of her mouth and smiled ✖ Her body was covered in those temporary tattoos you get free with popsicles and her skin was the brownest I've ever seen ✖ Her hair hung blacker than black, tangled with sand and salt, damp ✖ One of her hands squeezed my brother's buttock ✖ I didn't even think about opening my mouth, and hid behind the rocks just as Pato turned around ✖ I went back to the beach wearing a huge smile ✖ The rest of them asked: What's the deal, Nancy? ✖ I ran toward the water ✖ Swam doggy paddle, up and down with the waves, and laughed and wriggled my legs ✖ ✖ From then on they were an item and every time we went there they'd drag themselves off to the rocks at least two or three times in the course of an afternoon ✖ They'd come back grinning from ear to ear

✖ ✖ ✖ ✖ ✖ ✖ ✖ ✖ ✖ ✖ ✖ ✖ ✖ ✖

The trips stopped for a while, of course, thanks to my mamá. Not long before Pato died, that same summer, as we were eating mandarins and saying goodbye to the sun, the sound of a car horn at our backs warned us it was all coming to an end ✖ Our parents were waiting for us, furious, and if mamá didn't lay into me right then and there it was because of the other kids and what their mothers might say if they knew ✖ She always used to tell us: This is our family, everyone else can keep their noses out ✖ ✖ ✖ As they dragged me over to the pickup I saw a Romany convoy in the distance, down in the gully. Three or four old cars ✖ Leaning against the hood and the doors in the evening light, ten thin silhouettes contemplated their surroundings. One of them had his hands on his hips and his shirt open. You could see his smile from afar. It was Jesulé, the same Romany man who'd been eyeing me all through Semana Santa the year before: I'd felt it settle on me, that same smile, in the midst of all the vendors and people crowding around to buy whatever was on sale ✖ Inside me, surprise and fear mingled with an uncontrollable heat. So much that even with mamá pulling my hair, Pato trying to placate her, and papá staring straight ahead as he drove incredibly slowly, the only thing I could think of was the Romany,

him, only him.

✖   ✖

I spent the rest of the summer locked in the house ✖ For the first few days I thought it was just because of the beach, but when I saw Pato again he took me by the shoulders and told me I ought to listen to our parents ✖ This time they're not overreacting, he said ✖ I asked him what had happened. At that time I had no idea what he'd been up to, and because I saw so little of him except on the holidays I was hurt that he'd side with our old mutual enemies ✖   ✖

(My mother our enemy because of her insanity, my father because of his inertia) ✖ Pato hugged me very tight and we trembled against each other. I felt how his spine stiffened, and it made me scared too. He told me that women's bodies had been showing up on the beach. Some of them washed in by the waves, others just buried up to their necks in the sand, their heads blue in the open air ✖ Five had shown up that week alone ✖ It's best if you stay home, Nancy. You're so pretty, and we've no idea who's behind it ✖ Everyone's shitting themselves. It got so bad the Romany took off for fear they'd be blamed. If you ask me it was guys from the big port, or maybe a bunch of mutants,[3] but Romany? ✖ We looked at each other

---

[3] Between the big port and Ch there were a bunch of little towns: the only big one, bigger even than Ch and set back from the coast, was a place that had been blessed by the arrival of progress: a few kilometers from the last houses on the outskirts of San Fermín they'd erected a coal-fired power plant that within ten years had devastated the countryside. The only people left there, the only ones who still hadn't taken off, were those who were too poor to leave their jobs at the plant ✖ Children were born with breathing difficulties, and over the years their bodies acquired an ashy color and the consistency of wet wool ✖ You could recognize them from afar by the way they walked, always exhausted, pigeon-chested and shoulders slumping, and to top it off, dry, feverish eyes ✖ When the first refugees arrived at school some good Samaritan dreamed up the nickname and that was that: from then on they were, all of them, mutants.

and laughed, thinking how absurd it was, the idea
that a gang of mutants might have forced themselves
on a woman. Not even a group of twenty of them
could have raped the weakest girl in the neighbor-
hood, the littlest of little misses ✖ ✖ ✖ ✖ ✖ Either
way, my brother concluded, mutants, guys from the
big port, or even Romany, I don't want to lose you,
Nancy. Just lay low here, take the opportunity to
look after mamá and papá and be happy you're alive
✖ I looked at him adoringly, taking his advice to
heart without being entirely convinced ✖ That said,
the idea of never seeing the Romany man again left
me feeling sick. Now that I was fixated on having
Jesulé between my legs, what had previously been
nightmares had become a more interesting mixture.
In every dream, either before or after the Romany
arrived to enslave me, he would visit: the door would
open and, eyes closed, pretending to be asleep, I'd feel
him climb onto the bed and cling to me from behind
like an octopus ✖ I'd let him give it to me slowly,
sighing and squeezing my thighs, as a rash broke
out all up my back from the chafing of his unshaved
face ✖ The same smell that had terrified me before
was now ambiguous, it made me wake up anxious,
my nipples swollen, my still undeveloped nipples, of
whose shape I was very ashamed. My little breasties,
I used to call them, laughing to myself, looking at
myself naked in the bathroom mirror, pinching them
✖ ✖ I never in my life experienced greater pleasure
than I did in those dreams ✖ Not even later, when
I lost my virginity to Jesulé himself and experienced

actual sex ✖ In that moment, standing next to Pato, I was just as turned on as I was in my daydreams about the Romany, and I thought, it's not fair it's not fair it's not fair! Those rapists took him away from me, they sent him to the desert with his pots and pans and his face like a greyhound ✖ I hugged my brother again and another anxiety descended on me: soon I'd have to watch him leave once more for the big port ✖ I felt like everyone was running away from me except for my miserable mother, my madre mala ✖ The second year I spent without him was a black time, bitter. If during the summer the house had always seemed empty, after March it was practically a graveyard ✖ My papá came and went from work like a robot ✖ Sometimes he'd bring home his account books and computer and spend the night in front of a template, adding up numbers ✖ The only person who was always there was her, and all she did was clean things and tell me what a piece of shit her family was, how happy I should feel for having been born into a well-run home, where the Lord had been generous with money and education, not like in the other households in this town, full of envious idiots dying of hunger ✖ She had a face like a goosefish. Downturned lips. Hair all over the place. Wearing something between pyjamas and a cleaner's uniform. A different grimace depending on the occasion. Some people received tense, smooth smiles, smiles that barely made it across the threshold, melting back as soon as she was inside the house. Other people, her own family, got the crusts, the leftovers from a sleepless night: puffy eyes, dripping nose, face full of anguish. Stressing about everything being just right, the fish being well seasoned, there being enough mashed potato, nobody having to fill up on bread, Ch's young people remaining uncorrupted by the nightlife, the Temple being rebuilt before the Second Coming.

✖

That night, while all that and god knows what else was going on behind my mother's grotesque mask, was the last time Pato ate with us. THE LAST SUPPER.[4]

✖ It was like we all knew in advance, because my mamá didn't make a scene for once and my papá didn't pull that idiotic face of his as he chewed in silence ✖ No, that night a calm flooded the table and made me go still, cold, despite that damn heat which seemed to loosen itself from the walls as soon as the sun set.

---

[4] Judas wasn't there though, or maybe he himself was Judas, the Pato of the future, of a couple of weeks later, Pato crossing the desert at dawn, Pato dancing among the sweaty bodies in Hurricane Bar or Godzilla, Pato laughing with his friends, trying to get it on with any young flower who lets her guard down, Pato with three grams of coke up his nose, shivering with regret, black as a Chinchorro mummy, soulless ✖ ✖ ✖

✖ ✖ After dessert Pato's friends came by to pick him up. By the time we were alone I could tell a new ten-month-long nightmare was beginning ✖ My papá's eyes told me I wasn't the only one who was worried ✖ Mamá, showing her sweet side, which was even weirder than her usual uproar, took us by the hands and said: Read us something, Nancy. Let's go to sleep with something beautiful to reflect on in our hearts

And so I picked out a Daily Bread card:

Yea, a man may say, Thou hast faith, and I have works: shew me thy faith without thy works, and I will shew thee my faith by my works. Thou believest that there is one God; thou doest well: the devils also believe, and tremble.
Epistle of Saint James, 2:18–19

✖ I didn't understand what it meant ✖ I doubt my parents did either, but it wasn't for us to ask questions, rather to clear the table, wash the dishes, and bury our faces in our pillows.

The next morning I noticed my brother was missing from the seat next to my papá in the pickup on the way to the big port ✖ And that was that ✖ I didn't find out what had happened till the following week, from a classmate. My parents kept it from me ✖ We were walking from the school gates to the estate where we both lived, and Camila said to me: Pato's missing, Nancy. And they've taken Sandra to the big port, to juvie ✖ We were sucking on little tubes of frozen juice, the ones that leave your hands and tongue very red or green or blue, and I felt like I was going to die ✖ I stopped and looked at her, dead serious. She walked on another half block till she realized I was no longer following. I crossed the street, not taking my eyes off her, and ran home. My mamá wasn't there, so I went out to walk on the beach for a while. I looked at the seagulls, felt the sand under my feet, and asked myself: What the fuck is going on.

Where is Pato.
✖ where

✖ ✖
✖ ✖   ✖   ✖   ✖
       ✖   ✖   ✖   ✖

I didn't dare ask my papá till a couple of days later when I went to the big port with him to pick up his checks ✖ That whole time we'd been going around the house in complete silence. I was supposed to think Pato was looking for somewhere to stay in the big port, and that mamá was going back and forth to help ✖ ✖ ✖ ✖ When my papá parked the car in front of the office I took his hand and said to him, looking at my toes twitching inside my sandals: Pato's dead, isn't he? ✖ He didn't know what to say. He just hugged me and gave me a two-luca note ✖ ✖ We still don't know ✖ ✖ Go and buy a kilo of rolls and spend the change on whatever you want ✖ ✖ He said this with a warning look that made it clear there was nothing more to be said on this topic ✖ And so it was.

I decided to go to the farthest bakery I could think of, and as I crossed the streets of the big port town—a horrible place, then and now, full of fat people and new cars—I saw *him*: with all his brothers, helping some kids from a senatorial candidate's campaign team build a stage in the town square ✖ I realized for the first time that the place was overrun with election propaganda ✖ From their trucks full of posters the Romany were coordinating things backstage. He was hanging from the light tower, shirtless, copper-colored from dirt and sunshine ✖ Our eyes met and he smiled at me ✖ I ran to the bakery, squeezing my legs tight together. I had to ask to use their toilet. Inside, I laughed, running my finger over a saint's card bearing the image of St. Jude the Apostle, like I was blind ✖ I went back quickly, not daring to look at him again, but feeling him there, always in wait, just like at the market during Semana Santa ✖ ✖ ✖ And when I was on my way home, he reached his hand out over everyone's heads, holding a caramel apple, trembling ✖ ✖ ✖ ✖ ✖ ✖ ✖

Then he winked and ran off with my smile ✖
✖ ✖ ✖

I spent hours thinking about him, locked up in the
house. More bodies had been found, all women,
along the length of the beach, so my mamá's para-
noia had tripled, though I always thought the whole
murdered-women thing was an excuse to keep me
on a short leash ✖ One day, for example, when we
were in the middle of doing the beans, she said to me,
sinking her fingers into my hair: You better watch
yourself, 'cause you're ripe now, you little brat, like a
flower open to the wasps, to the pack on the hunt,
and I don't want you getting knocked up ✖ I kept
quiet and went on peeling and peeling, concentrating
on the bag. Doubt gnawed at me: How could I be
sure the woman didn't suspect something? Could I
not relax even in my daydreams? ✖ Old women can
tell just by looking at you. Mamá could tell, and she
spelled it out to me: Your hair's all shiny, and so's the
skin on your face and neck.

✖ ✖

✖ It'll be worse when you get your period ✖ ✖ ✖
I hope you never get it ✖ God willing ✖ ✖ I said
nothing, just sighed ✖

You're not even a woman yet and already you're going around like a bitch in heat, you little piece of shit.

✖

And I, the Lord God, caused a deep sleep to fall upon Adam;
and he slept, and I took one of his ribs and closed up the
flesh in the stead thereof; And the rib which I, the Lord
God, had taken from man, made I a woman, and brought
her unto the man. And Adam said: This I know now is
bone of my bones, and flesh of my flesh; she shall be called
Woman, because she was taken out of man. Therefore shall a
man leave his father and his mother, and shall cleave unto
his wife; and they shall be one flesh. And they were both
naked, the man and his wife, and were not ashamed.
The Pearl of Great Price, Joseph Smith

I'd already given up on him. I was barely sleeping, tossing between the sheets, the mattress beginning to sag from the damp ✖ My body was burning ✖

But the devils, in their perpetual circling, wanted my mamá to run away, to leave forever, to live in the big port ✖ And after a week living alone with my papá I ran into the Romany man outside the house, on a day as sad as any previous day.

I'd overslept, so instead of going to school I spent the morning watching cartoons. As I turned on the tap in the front patio to water the flowerpots, that same feeling from my dreams, from that time in the town square in the big port. It hit me in the knees and rose up to my belly button ✖ Like someone had rubbed mentholatum all over me.

    ✖ ·✖   ✖   ✖   ✖
✖   ✖   ✖   ✖

There he was, standing in the street, smoking.

✖✖✖ I opened the gate ✖✖✖ ✖✖✖ He entered serenely ✖✖✖ We went into the house and he fucked me on the tiles of the living room floor ✖✖✖✖ Afterward he washed his face and left ✖✖✖✖

✖

✖ The same thing happened about three more times, until it started to get really risky and no longer made any sense. The last time he came to see me I actually spent thinking about what Pato had said to me before he got lost or died, and about my papá's anxiety, and I lay there practically motionless, reliving the family tragedy in my head: my mamá, apparently worn out by it all, had used a trip to the big port to ask around about Pato's body as an opportunity to move in with her sister ✖ She couldn't stand life in Ch ✖ According to her it was a shady, dead-end town where everyone was either drunk or jealous ✖ Jesulé writhed on top of me ✖ She couldn't leave without making a scene: mamá mala completely lost it, shouting at papá bueno while throwing clothes into a duffel bag. She called him everything under the sun: eejit, fucking queer,

poor sad loser ✖ And so it went.

✖ I stood in the doorway and asked them what the matter was. Then, seizing the moment, shouted: And what the hell's going on with Pato?

They looked around at me, frightened.

Not even they knew what was going on.

✖ Papá was sitting on the edge of the bed crying silently. Snot was hanging down past his chin ✖ Mamá already had her bag over her shoulder ✖ I sat down next to papá on the bed and hugged him. The only thing he did during the whole episode was rest his hairy hand on my shoulder and say: She's staying with me. You can do what you like, *darling*, but Nancy's not going anywhere ✖ ✖ ✖ ✖ ✖ ✖ ✖ ✖ And so it went ✖ Mamá left and never came back to Ch ✖ Papá shut himself away and worked, worked with such contained fury it almost killed him. In the three weeks between the sudden separation and the arrival of his saviors he lost a lot of weight. He spent whole nights watching TV ✖ As for me, in truth I was more worried about my meetings with Jesulé, terrified of the idea that one of the women from the estate would catch on to what we were up to, than I was about my papá, or about what life would be like now that, against all odds, we had become what they referred to in school as a broken family, dysfunctional ✖ Papá bueno, papá tonto, so good and so stupid that he'd die if it carried on like this, and there was nothing I could do ✖ I had my own things to think about. For example: every time Jesulé penetrated me I started bleeding, a lot, and I'd think: my period's started ✖ But he'd come close and smell it ✖ Then he'd say: It's like your cherry's growing back every time I pop it ✖ ✖ So I was worried not only about that but also about getting the blood stains out of my clothes, keeping the house clean, buying food, homework ✖

One morning I felt a jolt between my ears, elastic, like something in my brain had moved without causing any pain. After that, I gradually stopped caring so much about the Romany. Like when you're standing by the road and see a bus in the distance, and you turn your head slowly as it approaches, but before you've even had time to register its arrival it's already disappeared beyond the horizon ✖ ✖ Back then it felt like I only ever saw the nape of Jesulé's neck.

Third time's always the charm. He ejaculated between my neck and breasts and then left, this time without even washing: he simply pulled up his pants and backed out the open door, quiet as ever ✖ That's when I realized the only thing that really mattered was that my papá was working himself to death ✖ That while I rolled around in sin with the most delicious of sinners, the most pitiful of sinners was losing his grip on this world. He really was dying ✖

But inscrutable are the ways of the Lord, as they say around here, and in some ways my life illustrated the truth of that proverb: everyone in Ch knew my father read the Bible, though we never went to church of any kind ✖ For years, papá tonto was heaven's most sought-after new recruit ✖ We got a lot of home visits. He was so dense, though, that after a certain amount of awkwardness they'd all eventually abandon their attempts to win him over: priests, nuns, Jehovah's Witnesses, Baptists, Pentecostals, Methodists, Anabaptists, Mennonites. In truth they all paid us a visit but always left with their tails between their legs ✖ ✖ Papá would listen to them, then ask a few well-aimed, specific questions, as though they were sat around the table talking about geometry or shipping costs, and by about the time the evangelist was answering the second to last question it became obvious the house was a barren wasteland, or at best a forest where the only things that grew were things my father cultivated on the direct advice of Scripture. It was almost fun to predict these scenes: the house felt refreshed, and we were all actually quite proud of our father, and he was proud of himself, he who usually said little but took advantage of these opportunities to lubricate the spirit via the tongue ✖ A giant of God ✖ In any case, that morning when the Mormons managed to get into the house and interest my papá in the teachings of the Prophet and the possibility of becoming a god in a future life, on a faraway planet, that morning was so, so gray that to tell the truth if it had been the postman who'd arrived, or a knife sharpener, the old man would still have been taken in, some way or other ✖ The lucky Brothers, rewarded for their stubbornness, were named Bryan and Josías.

Elder McLean

THE CHURCH OF
JESUS CHRIST
OF LATTER DAY SAINTS

Elder Moroni

THE CHURCH OF
JESUS CHRIST
OF LATTER DAY SAINTS

Bryan was born and raised in Salt Lake City, in North America. Josías was Mexican, though he'd been born in the outskirts of a Mormon community in Nuevo León. They were classic missionaries: twenty-something years old, a little on the plump side, clean, with short-sleeved shirts, black ties, name badges, and backpacks faded from the sun. They invited themselves in, encountering no resistance from this man whose wife had abandoned him, who was carrying around the pain of a son missing, probably dead, and there the two of them stayed ✖ My papá looked so animated that I sat down and listened, or pretended to anyway ✖ I thought about my last visit from the Romany and realized that a new era was beginning. I quietly relived our antics in the living room, while around the table they discussed Jesus's travels through America; the disputes between the Nephites and the Lamanites, descendants of the tribes of Israel who had arrived on the new continent on an ark made according to divine instructions; the appearance of God the Father and God the Son to Joseph Smith in a forest in the United States; etcetera, etcetera ✖ I tensed my thighs against my groin and those moments of uncertainty, sweet uncertainty I'd spent with the Romany, blossomed inside me.

I tangled together my thin white legs and felt like I was in love ✖ Strangely alien to myself ✖ Like my soul had been abducted, vacuumed out of my uterus, and was contemplating Jesulé's back and buttocks from the ceiling as he made his wild assaults on my body ✖ The whole thing was always a glossy, fetid mess that left me exhausted but happy, expanded ✖ Then with another jolt I was back to that morning when my papá secretly devoted his soul to the Latter Day Saints: he let them talk, asked many more questions than usual. The minutes ticked by and for the first time since I'd been living with him he actually took the day off work ✖ At first I couldn't tell from his face if the Brothers' words were actually sinking in or if he'd just found himself a little bit of calm, bracketed off from the rest of life, in the noises issuing from the clean mouths and the perfect teeth of those creatures who had come so far. But the Brothers really had managed to get my papá interested ✖ ✖ The Word of God had done its work, and via those missionaries with their tanned necks and yellowing armpits it moved him, drawing him slowly into their embrace ✖ Damn the Word and damn the sneaking Truth, taking advantage so cruelly, so mockingly of a man who up until a few minutes ago believed he had no soul ✖ ✖ I felt it: it was there, in the atmosphere, its body soaking into everything ✖ The missionaries' every sentence was a long, seductive limb proffered to my father like a glass of water to a mule driver in the desert ✖ The Word, that tantalizing loin: the Word Bryan, with his broad, slumping body, his serious but somehow cheerful gaze. The Word Josías with his impressive knowledge of the Bible and his ability to make subtle, speedy connections between the Book of Mormon and a load of other texts I'd never heard of ✖ The siren call of the Word ✖ And me, the last death rattle of my mental encounter with the Romany slipping down my spine, sitting next to them at the table, swinging my legs. I felt like God's Echo had permeated the foundations of the house.

When the table was groaning under piles of leaflets and they'd extracted a promise from my father to come and have a look around the temple, I decided that if I was going to keep my head I had to get out of there ✖ I stood up and, as I ran to the kitchen, told them I was going out to buy bread and something to eat for lunch ✖

✖

✖

As I was about to slam the door I realized nobody had stopped me: Josías and Bryan were still talking to my papá, showing him maps of the universe, confirming that today's wars were signs of the end times, comparing them with passages from Isaiah, excited, all of them

And he said, Oh let not the Lord be angry, and I will speak
yet but this once: Peradventure ten shall be found there.
And he said, I will not destroy it for ten's sake.
Genesis 18:32

And so papá tonto became a Saint: papá santo ✖ Papá
santo behaved exactly the same as papá tonto, except
that now he smiled, and things revolved around him
✖ Apart from that, at first nothing much seemed
to have changed: I still had to go to school, I could
still skip religion classes and sit alone on the patio
eating ramitas or ice cream while the bible-bashing
evangelical boys in my class—likewise exempt from
learning about the Roman Catholic church—tossed
a ball around ✖ The girls, who all had biblical names,
gathered in a circle at the edge of the sports field and
then walked around the courtyard, forming a kind
of procession ✖ Their hair and their dresses were
very long. They seemed to be disgusted by everything
except what was inside their own homes and their
temples ✖ They might've considered talking to me
before but now they rejected me entirely. They all
knew: about my mamá, about Pato, and also that
whenever I could, even knowing it was fucking stupid, I went down to the beach with the other kids ✖
✖ ✖ ✖ ✖ And at the beach was the devil. The

desert had once been the seafloor but the beach now marked its final reaches. And in the desert the Lord had been tempted ✖ ✖   ✖   ✖   ✖
✖   ✖   ✖   ✖   ✖   ✖   ✖
✖   Being with me meant being with death, and for them there was only

✖ Resurrection ✖

In a sense I think they intuited my end, they saw this drugged corpse haunting them from the future ✖ Nancy Cancer floating above Nancy recently Eve ✖
✖ The art of learning to tolerate those who do not tolerate you ✖

After mamá left, it was up to me to keep the house in order because papá santo still didn't know how to cook or bleach a bath clean ✖ ✖ ✖ When I got home from school I'd change my clothes and scrub away happily, especially after the Romany stopped coming around ✖ I had energy: I could kneel for hours on the floor, getting the tiles impossibly shiny. And besides, I liked it because it was like doing my own personal stations of the cross: slowly, expectantly, I'd approach the areas of the house where Jesulé and I had done it. I'd linger over them, giving it my all, until my fingers throbbed tight and wrinkled and my swollen ripped cuticles, skin flapping, dripped blood ✖

One day while I was cleaning, more turned on than ever, they bled a lot more than was normal ✖

Black blood, ten big drops, trembling ✖ New blood, thickening as it fell ✖ The drops, little balls of mercury, danced with each other until they formed the face of Christ ✖

It spoke to me:
Nancy Cortés, why did you abandon me? ✖

That was all ✖

I answered:
Lord, why do you ask that?

✖ HIM: Your father is writhing in pain between his work and false idols, and you're here, Nancy… you're here…dragging yourself across the floor like a bitch with distemper…

✖ The Lord looked sad, more sad than usual ✖ Even more than in church, where he's shown crucified, his side open like a piece of honeycomb ✖

As I stammered, cloth in hand, the drops went back to being a formless puddle ✖ And the puddle evaporated at the same time as the wounds around my nails closed up ✖ And with that Christ left me ✖ The light changed in the room. Maybe the sun went behind a cloud. Probably. I don't know ✖ I never told papá santo, because that night he came home smiling from ear to ear. I thought: Why piss on his parade? ✖ ✖ Didn't Solomon erect his wives' foreign idols on the stones of the Temple, in the very presence of the Lord? And what about the Jews on Mount Sinai with the golden calf? ✖ ✖ ✖ I didn't ask why he was smiling. I just served him his appetizer and a glass of juice, and we ate, with me lost in thought while he read a book that rested next to his plate ✖ The Daily Bread had been replaced by him reading a Latter Day Saints volume to himself ✖ Every time he turned the page he'd lift his head and offer me an affectionate look ✖ The plates won't wash themselves, mija, he said eventually, perhaps unsettled that I hadn't asked him about his silence, nor about what he was reading ✖

I cleared the table willingly, pleased to see him like that, devouring the Word one bit at a time, so eager ✖

His method bore spiritual fruit. Papá santo, now two months old, seemed never to feel alone, never to need anyone else ✖ He smiled like an idiot, like he was floating in neoprene, and devoted himself humbly to his days on earth ✖

And I came to understand that mamá mala running away had truly been a blessing for us all.

✖ ✖ ✖ ✖ ✖ ✖ ✖ ✖

I saw the Latter Day Saints Brothers again not long after ✖ One morning a couple of weeks later the dean of discipline came to find me in the classroom and said: Your father's here for you ✖ I gathered my things and left. He was waiting for me in the pickup. Bryan and Josías were there too, in the back seat ✖

✖ We're going to see your tío in C, papá said to me. He's just lost his job, so he could do with a prayer and a visit from the family.

✖ I hugged my backpack between my knees in the passenger seat and fell asleep as we were leaving Ch ✖

C was a horrible place where I hadn't been more than about five times. There were hardly any young people, and most adults worked in the pork processing plant on the edge of town ✖ There was no public transportation, only shuttle buses bearing the logo of a smiling pig wearing a crown perched between her ears ✖ Like this:

One day one of the pigs got sick. A strange flu spread, mutating uncontrollably, and within two weeks more than 1,500 people were out of work, among them my tío ✖ 12,000 pigs had to be slaughtered ✖ We followed it on the TV over the course of three weeks, and for some reason I never thought of tío Aarón when they showed images of journalists wearing face masks, or workers building barricades out of trash and rubble, or the army evacuating the area ✖ ✖ ✖ ✖ ✖ ✖ Then there were reports comparing the plants to concentration camps: gigantic pigs rolling around in their own shit, shrieking, pissing themselves in terror ✖ ✖ ✖ ✖ Everyone was talking about it in town, and we were once again united by a dead calm: a calm that came with the realization that Ch was not C ✖

You had to pass the processing plant on the way into C and, even though we closed the windows miles in advance, we could barely see the columns of smoke from its chimneys before my papá stopped the car abruptly so we could get out and vomit ✖ All of us ✖ It was unbearable ✖ ✖ I understood the silence that Tim would only reluctantly break if I asked him about the fish processing plant ✖ ✖ ✖ If I really insisted, the gringo would lift his fingers to his brow and say: I can still smell it in here ✖ All these years it's been the same ✖ Living inside this head stinking of fish shit, fish guts, chopped flesh seasoned with sweat and salt ✖ ✖ ✖ And now

I'm remembering being there that day, trembling, my stomach turning and my throat constricting: the pigs were leaving this world reduced to ashes and they weren't going to go without a warning ✖ ✖ ✖ ✖ ✖ ✖ ✖ ✖ ✖ ✖

I thought about the ten plagues God sent the Egyptians in the film *The Ten Commandments* and then about another animated film I saw when I was little ✖ I can still just about sing a couple of songs from that one ✖ ✖ ✖ ✖ ✖ In one of them Moses's father-in-law, Jethro, talks about how beautiful Creation is, like a tapestry in which everyone lives in harmony, according to a plan ✖ ✖ ✖ ✖ ✖ ✖ ✖ ✖ ✖ ✖ But Creation was nowhere to be seen here ✖ The twists of smoke rising into the sky were souls writhing ✖ ✖ ✖ ✖ Papá santo put his fingers down his throat and tried to keep vomiting, but none of us had anything left inside to ease the feeling any-more ✖ Crouching down, crying tears of nausea, the Brothers encircled him. Tried to stay composed ✖ ✖

We got back into the car and approached the plant: at the entrance to the complex three special forces offi-cers stood guard against a huge scratched-up door, submachine guns in hand and gas masks on their faces ✖ Two guanacos were keeping an immense pack of dogs at bay, more dogs than I've ever seen in one place before or since ✖ Skinny and starving, goose-pimpled, foaming at the mouth ✖ Bryan and Josías were in shock, holding hands. In between retches they repeated what I assumed were psalms or reflections of the Prophet ✖ I thought, they must be thinking: Thousands of miles on an evangelizing mission only to arrive and find ourselves, after all that, contemplating a scene from hell ✖ ✖ ✖ ✖ And so it was ✖

We found my tío sitting in his living room in the dark ✖ We had to force the door open to get in ✖ He was sunk in an armchair sipping from an almost empty bottle of pisco ✖ He trembled when he saw us, and as soon as the light reached his body he leaped up and ran over to a dark corner: WHO ARE YOU? he asked over and over again ✖ Papá santo replied in a defeated voice:

Aarón, man, it's me, your brother

✖ My tío seemed not to hear him, and papá had to hug him, look him right in the eye, and repeat in his ear:
Aarón, man, it's me, your brother
✖ ✖

They sent me off to try and find an open kiosk or grocery store where we could buy some food. Bryan and Josías took down the boards covering the windows and swept the floors while the Cortés brothers murmured quietly. They were barely looking at each other ✖ It was as though they'd never met ✖ I came back empty-handed after half an hour, thankful we had the car so we could get out of there as quickly as possible ✖ The town was pretty much abandoned: there wasn't a single door or window open ✖ Not the church nor the police station nor the haberdashery nor the bakery nor the convenience store ✖ The streets were infested with dogs, sprawled in the slices of shade alongside white and blue adobe houses, riding out the heat ✖ No people around ✖ Only the echoes of my own footsteps. My shadow touching the street corners, slipping down unpaved passageways and past disemboweled trash bags ✖ ✖ ✖

My tío couldn't even take a shower (there was no water), couldn't eat (there was no bread), and I couldn't find a single trace of life (there was none), so we went back to Ch in the car, the Cortés brothers in the front seats ✖ I didn't know what was worse: the smell of thousands of dead pigs permeating the place at large, or the bodily soup tío Aarón was exuding up close ✖ I played with the window, raising and lowering it, negotiating with the stink ✖

The Mormon Brothers were totally dazed, and for the whole trip, since we'd gotten out to vomit really, they didn't open their mouths except to pray, and then only in very quiet voices ✖ When we passed the plant again, my papá stopped the pickup and approached the armed cops, holding a tissue dipped in Flaño cologne to his face ✖ It dripped, grazing his leg ✖ Papá santo raised his free hand and shouted something that I think must have been something like "We come in peace" or "Pharoah, let my people go." Who knows ✖ One of the cops pointed his machine gun at him and that was that: papá ran to the pickup and we sped off petrified back to Ch ✖

On the way tío Aarón relaxed a bit and told us what had happened ✖ First the pigs getting sick, then dying ✖ People's initial fury, the protests, the violence in the streets ✖ Then the arrival of a Minister of State and the special forces ✖ When the people of C refused to send representatives to meet with her, the Minister laid down her curse: Never again will we remember you in the capital, she said, according to my tío ✖

Then the slow exodus toward the horizon, the sea

✖ ✖ Now C was deserted, and the few people who'd had to stay, like my tío, spent their time locked inside ✖ Recently I went out to look for food, he told us, and I found an old couple, the Arayas, dead in their home ✖ Their flesh was tight, like they'd been made into jerky ✖ I took the few things that remained in their kitchen and went back into confinement ✖ ✖

At night, tío Aarón told us, it's impossible to sleep. Impossible. All the dogs in C, and there were always way more dogs than people, howling, barking, flooding the city with their pain.

✖ ✖ Six thousand dogs, or thereabouts, all dying of hunger, eating the adobe off the walls, eating each other ✖ ✖ ✖

And Isaac answered and said unto Esau, Behold, I have made him thy lord, and all his brethren have I given to him for servants; and with corn and wine have I sustained him: and what shall I do now unto thee, my son? And Esau said unto his father, Hast thou but one blessing, my father? bless me, even me also, O my father. And Esau lifted up his voice, and wept. And Isaac his father answered and said unto him, :

Genesis 27:37–39

Your brother is dead and you turned out to be a slut ✖ Get out. I don't have any children anymore ✖

That's what he said ✖

I arrived at the big port by coach ✖ I was still crying over papá santo's curse ✖ Mamá mala was waiting for me at the station. Fat and sporting a tracksuit ✖ She stroked my hair, pleased. She enjoyed seeing me cry. We took a colectivo to the outskirts of town where she was living, miles from the sea, up near the ravines ✖ There she gave me something to eat and said: If you want to stay here you'll have to work, we don't put people up just for the hell of it ✖ Manuel's given everything to get where he is ✖ And quite right too

✖ ✖ What about my tía? I thought about asking, but then it hit me: her sister, if she ever existed, was no more ✖ Deep down I always suspected they weren't close enough for mamá to just up and stay with her like that ✖ Mamá usually only took the initiative if there was something in it for her ✖ Some pleasure or some gain ✖ The rest of the time she had a face like a butt ✖

Four days later Manuel turned up from his stint down the mine. He was a short man with a gut molded from beer and white bread ✖ He looked at my legs appreciatively, then looked at my mamá, and to make himself totally clear, said: This kid's not living with us. Then he said directly to me, looking me straight in the eye, in the same tired, dry tone: We wait till the Pastor calms down and then we send her back ✖ ✖ ✖ ✖

✖ ✖ ✖ ✖ ✖ ✖ ✖   ✖   ✖   ✖
✖ ✖ ✖   ✖ ✖ ✖

My papá had been busy with work. Some uncertainty about the future, about reality itself, had stretched across the whole of the north, and in city after city, town after town, something had happened ✖ Though nobody knew exactly what it was ✖ The Minister was traveling through the desert announcing decisions. Mainly death sentences that she tried to pass off as blessings, or sometimes as warnings ✖ San Fermín bagged itself a new coal-fired power station, which came with bonds for anyone who wanted to go back and live there ✖ There's nothing to worry about, she reassured everyone with a pearly smile: environmental studies have proven the project's viability ✖ She was surrounded by some two hundred women who were obviously not from San Fermín. The same women who surrounded her at every public event televised and broadcast in the north. All of them smiling, holding printed placards, so fat that between their chests and their groins there was just one great expanse of flesh sliced in half by their pants or the elastic of their skirts ✖ ✖ ✖ ✖

✖ The Minister spouted nonsense and they all dutifully repeated it ✖ And so the curse of the north spread ✖

Tío Aarón, who'd moved in with us, spent all day in front of the TV watching this quasi-invasion like he was in exile from a lost civil war ✖ I'd get home from school and find him sitting on the sofa eating celery or drinking tea, his eyes fixed on the screen ✖ I'd cook him something more filling and the three of us would have lunch together. Him, me, and the TV ✖
✖ ✖ ✖ ✖ ✖ ✖ ✖ ✖ ✖ ✖ ✖
✖ ✖ ✖ ✖ ✖ ✖ ✖ ✖ ✖ ✖ ✖

In the afternoons I could do what I wanted. One day Tania came up to me after PE and said:
We're going to Playa Roja. A bunch of gringos are taking us ✖ I went home to

grab my things and get changed, then ran to join the rest of the group ✖ There were no boys

✖ That's how the gringos want it and the gringos are paying, Tania explained with a shrug ✖ Fifteen minutes later two white jeeps and a blue van appeared ✖ ✖ They honked at us, we crossed the road and got in ✖

There were about twelve of us in all. In the van three men sat up front: the driver was a young skinny Chilean guy ✖ The other two were hilarious fifty-somethings. They weren't fat, but they had little bulbous bellies. They wore their cotton shirts open, revealing pale, hairy chests. The more talkative of the two, who turned out to be a Canadian named Steven, had crab-red arms, neck, and face. The other one was named Gordon and was a bit darker-skinned: base-ball cap, round glasses, hairs on his neck ✖

They handed out cans of beer and turned up the reggaetón ✖ The girls sipped from their cans and answered questions from our hosts. They laughed at their jokes, at their bad Spanish, at the smell of oranges and cigars permeating the van ✖ ✖ I gave my beer to a girl named Juana, though she made them call her Jeanette, and concentrated on looking out at the desert.

When we arrived at Playa Roja we girls ran off at once to the wreck ✖ It was called that because it had been rusting for years, since before we were born, probably before our parents were born even ✖ Steven and Gordon joined the rest of the men: six or seven of them, not one under forty ✖ The driver, who never wanted to tell us his name, set about erecting an umbrella and unfolding tables, dragging coolers over, setting up tripods ✖ The gringos watched us bathing near the boat, swimming doggy paddle around it, jumping and laughing ✖ Through the splashing and the foam, half-blinded by the sun, we could just make them out: they lit each other's cigarettes, rubbed suntan lotion or coconut oil into their hairy shoulders, and knocked their drinks together in quiet good humor ✖ ✖ What is it these guys want? somebody asked ✖ Vero, who was by far the oldest, though still a sophomore because she'd been held back, said:

Nothing, just chill a while. I think they're filming around here and wanted to get to know the place. Get to know some girls ✖ ✖

That afternoon we ate chicken and watermelon ✖ There was also beer and apricot wine. And prickly pears and lemon-lime flavored vodka ✖ ✖ The gringos went around introducing themselves, and when we were all stretched out, all twenty of us, next to the table, on a sea of mats and pillows, someone suggested we improvise a film ✖

Tania was shivering from cold, her goosefleshed skin tight and dark, covered in droplets: How much are you gonna pay us though? she asked suddenly ✖

The gringos looked at each other and Gordon said: Depends what you want to do ✖

A bald guy wearing nothing but a ridiculous pair

of fuchsia speedos took out a plastic canister meant for rolls of film, and lifted the white tip of a little scoop up to his nose so delicately it made us laugh ✖ ✖

We'll sort that out after, don't worry about the money: help yourself to whatever you want, ladies, said Steven ✖ Gordon, making the most of the situation, sat one of the girls between his legs and took out a bag full of marijuana buds. Once he'd rolled himself a joint and taken a few deep drags the drugs began to circulate ✖ ✖ ✖

✖ Two of the men filmed, the rest of us just concentrated on having a good time

✖ It was fun, because I didn't do anything that afternoon, or any other afternoon either.

✖ It was fun, because I'd thought, at the beginning, that the whole thing was a form of prostitution, a kind of trade-off: they brought food and drugs and a bit of cash for us to take home, and we brought our bodies ✖ ✖ But it wasn't like that ✖ Those who wanted to do something would do it, and those who didn't, didn't ✖ In fact I think it was only a couple of times that one of the girls ended up screwing a gringo ✖

It was fun, because most of the time we just swam, and ran naked holding hands with the men, and ate lying around under the awning ✖ Occasionally they'd run their rough hands over a leg or a back, but the attempt was so courteous, so delicate, that we didn't know what to think ✖ Usually we laughed. Some girls would stick out their tongue, biting down on it, jumpy from everything they'd snorted ✖ ✖

✖ ✖

✖ ✖

The gringos did jerk off in front of us, though, a lot. Maybe they were too stoned to try anything: they'd lie there like iguanas, belly buttons about to pop, their dicks throbbing semi-erect, peeping out from one side of their trunks or speedos ✖ The gentleness and courtesy of their advances robbed us of all our shame and also all our fear. They were strange, but kind ✖

✖ I managed to go maybe five times before papá realized I was spending all afternoon out of the house ✖   ✖   ✖   His suspicion was confirmed when he got home a couple of hours early from work and found tío Aarón alone in front of the screen ✖ ✖ What's more, in my absence tío had been on the bottle again ✖ The house didn't function without me, so it was only a matter of time, really, until he figured it out ✖ That night I got back at half past nine, happy, a bit of cash in my pocket, but sober, because I never tried anything they offered us, not even a beer ✖ My papá took one look at me and understood. I don't know how, but he understood ✖ I went over to say hi, still breathless from the afternoon, acting all innocent ✖ As I went over I saw his eyes moisten: he ran to the bathroom and locked himself in ✖ ✖ I cooked some spaghetti, laid the table, and went to bed ✖ In the middle of the night the door opened and papá santo stuck his head around the door, his soul eating him alive, and said that tomorrow I was out on the street ✖ And so it was.

✖ ✖
✖
✖ ✖ ✖

After four days of living with mamá mala I realized that Manuel was so attracted to me that if I didn't get out of there quick I'd be in deep shit ✖ I was embarrassed because I hadn't done anything, quite the opposite: despite the heat I'd covered myself up completely, except for my hands and from the neck up ✖ ✖ I read the Bible and worked twice as hard as when we all lived together in Ch ✖

One day when I'd been sent into town to buy beer and meat someone called my name ✖ I turned around and there was Sandra ✖ Thin, bags under her eyes ✖ She peeled off from a group of girls gathered behind a car down an alleyway, and ran to hug me ✖ ✖ ✖ I bought her a popsicle and we talked

✖ ✖ I thought they had you locked up, amiga, I said to her. Sandra said that in theory they did, but that juvie had its own rules.

✖ You can go out in the morning but you gotta be back before eight at night if you don't want to end up without a bed ✖ And no bed means you don't get any sleep at all. Though really everyone shares two or three to a bed anyway, and even then there aren't enough ✖ ✖ Ending up without a bed is the worst ✖ Also, you gotta bring some cash back ✖ The guards are nasty old men, silent but sick in the head ✖

Most inmates smoke basuco or rock, some sniff glue or benzene ✖

Others whatever they can find ✖ The guards bring in the basuco themselves ✖ To earn money we set ourselves up here in these alleys, where we're not far from the dormitory building, and take care of whoever comes asking. Though mostly it's just guards or miserable old truck drivers.

Sandra was licking her Trululú very calmly, almost happily I'd say ✖ But when I asked her about Pato her face cracked. Brow hardened. She smiled at me without smiling. She was missing one of her front teeth. Her lips tightened and I saw how all her skin followed suit ✖

That motherfucker left us all alone. I don't want to talk about Patito ✖ ✖ I replied that I understood she was upset, it was eating me up inside too, but I needed to know details: My parents told me nothing, Sandra. I found out from Camila ✖ ✖ ✖ ✖ Details about what though? And what for? We'll never know what really happened to him. God knows what he was mixed up in, Nancy, she said. A couple of drops of Trululú were now running down her hand, dripping onto her leg. I knew she

was right and hugged her. We cried ✘ What more
was there to do? ✘ We talked about the good old
days in Ch and the people we loved. Naturally we
got onto the topic of the gringos. She asked me
what they smelled like. I replied that there were a
lot of smells: watermelon rind, fruit in the mouth,
tobacco, armpits, booze, marijuana ✘ But that for
me there was one base smell that kept all the others
in circulation: a mixture of farmyards and salt mines
✘ ✘ ✘ Anyone worth your time? ✘ I replied that
the group was always different, but that the last couple of times there were at least two or three younger
guys ✘ ✘ ✘ One of these was Tim, though I didn't
know it yet. He was super quiet, paying more atten-
tion to the camera and the beach than anything
else: tall, a ready smile, drooping eyebrows, and no
exhibitionism or drugs, though he drank and swam
a lot. While we splashed around with some fat guy
we watched him play the same games we used to
on the wreck, then disappear in a series of perfect
strokes till he was just a speck floating on the sea.
One time he came back just as the sun was setting,
and in that moment I am certain every one of us
thought he was the most beautiful man in the world
✘ Another time he didn't come back at all ✘ His
friends weren't even worried ✘ ✘ ✘ ✘ ✘ It was
things like that that revealed how utterly cold they
were. I felt surrounded by icicles ✘ As for Jesulé, I
didn't even mention him to her, perhaps as a form
of revenge, though it was only revenge by way of
indifference ✘ ✘ ✘ We had nothing more to say

to each other ✖ I remembered the beer and the meat, to keep Manuel in his sizeable belly, and ran off, promising I'd be back ✖ ✖ Sandra gave me a look like a wild dog, happy and sad at the same time, doubting me ✖

✖ ✖

✖

We never saw each other again, because I ran away the following morning after a heated argument between mamá and Manuel ✖ Arguing's one way of putting it anyway. The miner was quick with his fists and short-tempered, so when my mamá started yelling he just beat the shit out of her with his bare hands ✖ ✖ At the first dry thumps, I poked my head around the door, holding my breath, my eyes very wide, and saw my mamá on the bed, sprawled on her belly. Her mouth was almost dislocating it was open so wide, but no sound came out. Manuel was meting out blows without seeing where they fell, her back or her buttocks or her legs. His gaze moved between the nape of his woman's neck and the door ✖ ✖ ✖ I stayed long enough to witness a couple more blows, paralyzed, then went back to the sofa. Since there was no bolt on the door, I closed my eyes and repeated all the prayers I could remember until I fell asleep ✖

The next morning the miner was in the kitchen drinking wine from a blue tin mug ✖ Your mother's sick, he said, so you'll be looking after the house today ✖ I stared at the floor, at my bare feet balancing on the splintered floorboards, and said:

Ah

✖ ✖ ✖ Rancheras were playing on the radio. Outside the old ladies were heading to mass ✖ ✖ Swollen legs barely contained inside multiple pairs of tights. Withered flesh ✖ Flies starting to zip around the kitchen ✖ Manuel's heavy breathing ✖ The wine-crust on his swollen lips ✖ ✖ Go and get us some eggs and bread for breakfast, and a bottle of rum and three liters of Coke, he said, leaving a ten-luca note on the table ✖ He stretched and went out into the courtyard for a piss ✖

I spent the money on the first bus back to Ch and ran straight home ✖ My tío wasn't there, but this didn't seem to have stopped papá santo from dirtying everything in sight ✖ I took a shower and cleaned. That night, when the Pastor stuck his head around the door, he made a face like he thought he'd gone back in time ✖ I was reading the Gospel on the sofa in the living room ✖ I looked at him with joy and love and ran to hug him ✖ We cried and told each other everything ✖ ✖ I asked for his infinite forgiveness as I buried my face in his belly

✖ And so my father's curse came to an end, and for a while we went back to being happy

And it shall be, when he lieth down, that thou shalt mark the place where he shall lie, and thou shalt go in, and uncover his feet, and lay thee down; and he will tell thee what thou shalt do. And she said unto her, All that thou sayest unto me I will do.

Ruth 3:4–5

Once I was back we realized we could no longer be apart ✖ Tío Aarón had left one day without warning, with nothing but the clothes on his back, and since then my old man's only companions had been his calculation templates, the Latter Day Saints, the Word, and a bit of TV.

✖ ✖ ✖ I decided to become exactly the woman papá santo needed, the perfect daughter, a fitting complement for his love of the Word ✖ I studied the Old Testament, the Pauline epistles, and the Book of Mormon with a feigned interest that soon turned into actual enthusiasm ✖ I was so happy I wasn't even thinking about Sandra, or Jesulé, or even Pato ✖ Every time papá got home from work and found me reading, the table laid and the house clean, he said, looking emotional: There she is, my Every Day Saint ✖ Sure, the calm was maintained by a troubling silence ✖ One day papá santo said to me, as though he knew perfectly well that something had to be said: There are things it's better to erase from your mind, mijita. This world is a desert of crosses. You just have to keep your head down, have Faith, be happy ✖ ✖ Arm yourself like the Lion of Judah, walk calmly, without fear of pain or of making mistakes, until the Son decides: enough, enough now ✖

✖ ✖ It was such a pretty speech that I asked if I could visit the Church of the Saints as soon as possible ✖ I don't think you can if you haven't been baptized, he answered, but if you're really interested, for starters Sister Ruth can give you a tour of the temple ✖

✖ ✖ ✖ ✖ ✖ ✖ ✖ ✖ ✖ ✖ ✖ ✖ ✖ ✖ ✖ ✖ ✖ ✖
✖ ✖ ✖ ✖ ✖ ✖ ✖ ✖ ✖ ✖ ✖ ✖ ✖ ✖ ✖ ✖ ✖ ✖
✖ ✖ ✖ ✖ ✖ ✖ ✖ ✖ ✖ ✖ ✖ ✖ ✖ ✖ ✖ ✖ ✖ ✖
✖ ✖ ✖ ✖ ✖ ✖ ✖ ✖ ✖ ✖ ✖ ✖

✖ And so there we were: Sister Ruth and I. No images. Bare white walls, some flower pots, plenty of space and light ✖ She said: Questions after the video ✖ She pointed to a door to our right and in we went ✖ ✖ I sat down, accepted a glass of water, and spent the next twenty minutes learning about Joseph Smith ✖ When it finished I couldn't think of any questions and so we looked at each other in silence ✖ ✖ ✖ ✖ ✖ ✖ ✖ Then she invited me into the only other place the unbaptized were allowed to visit: she opened an immense door and we looked at a painting of Joseph Smith in the middle of a forest, facing away from us, kneeling in front of the Father and the Son who were looking out from among the clouds and light:

not a revelation, The Revelation ✖

Before I left Sister Ruth said: Come back whenever you like, Nancy. But come calmly ✖ ✖ ✖ ✖ ✖ ✖
✖ ✖ ✖ ✖ ✖ ✖ ✖ ✖ ✖ ✖

✖ ✖ ✖ I went home tired and happy. Papá santo hugged me and continued in his private trance, less excited than I thought he'd be ✖

I'm proud of you, hija, I wanted to hear.

But all I got was the calm and certainty of another day on this earth. And so on until we die ✖ ✖ ✖
✖ ✖ A universe with space for both Sandra and Ruth, both Tim and Jesulé, Noah's Ark and the boat at Playa Roja, my tío and the Minister, the dogs and the clouds, cactus forests and the tendons of drug mules ✖ ✖ ✖
✖ ✖ ✖ ✖
✖ ✖ ✖ ✖
✖ ✖ ✖ ✖ ✖ ✖ ✖ ✖ ✖ ✖ ✖
✖ ✖ ✖ ✖ ✖ ✖ ✖
✖ ✖ ✖
✖ ✖ ✖ ✖ ✖
✖ ✖
✖ ✖ ✖ ✖ ✖ ✖ ✖
✖ ✖ ✖ ✖ ✖ ✖
✖ ✖ ✖ ✖

✕ ✕ ✕ ✕ ✕ ✕ ✕ ✕ ✕ ✕ ✕ ✕ ✕ ✕ ✕ ✕ ✕ ✕
✕ ✕ ✕ ✕ ✕ ✕ ✕ ✕ ✕ ✕ ✕ ✕ ✕ ✕ ✕
✕ ✕ ✕

It's not that the gringos left one day, but rather that they simply never came back. At first we thought they'd gotten bored, though Tim later told me the main actor in their troupe had been possessed by a kind of miraculous energy and determination to work, so the rhythm of the team transformed: they went from wandering around in sad circles in the desert to racing against the clock, thanking their lucky stars every day that the actor's good humor remained undiminished ✕ ✕ One day he went completely to pieces, and the gringos brought him a couple of girls to ease his mood ✕ ✕ Tim told me this and it was horrible: horrible because I never knew, horrible because one of those girls committed suicide a couple of years later, horrible because no one, including my gringo, did anything.

✕ ✕ ✕ ✕ ✕ ✕ ✕ ✕ ✕ ✕ ✕ ✕ ✕ ✕ ✕ ✕ ✕ ✕
✕ ✕ ✕ ✕ ✕ ✕ ✕ ✕ ✕ ✕ ✕ ✕ ✕ ✕ ✕ ✕ ✕ ✕
✕ ✕ ✕ ✕ ✕ ✕ ✕ ✕ ✕ ✕

✕ ✕ ✕ ✕ ✕ ✕ ✕ ✕ ✕ ✕ ✕ ✕ ✕ ✕ ✕ ✕ ✕
✕ ✕ ✕ ✕ ✕ ✕ ✕ ✕ ✕ ✕ ✕ ✕ ✕ ✕ ✕ ✕ ✕ ✕
✕ ✕ ✕ ✕ ✕ ✕ ✕ ✕ ✕ ✕ ✕ ✕
　　　✕　　✕　　✕
　　　✕　　✕
　　　✕　　✕　　✕　　✕　　✕

For this cause God gave them up unto vile affections:
for even their women did change the natural use into
that which is against nature: And likewise also the men,
leaving the natural use of the woman, burned in their lust
one toward another; men with men working that which
is unseemly, and receiving in themselves that recompence
of their error which was meet. And even as they did not
like to retain God in their knowledge, God gave them
over to a reprobate mind, to do those things which are not
convenient

Romans 1:26–28

One twelfth of October my papá was let go from
the department store where he did the books ✖
When I got home from school he was sitting at
the table in the dining room with the Bible open
in front of him, his eyes wandering. He had both
palms pressed down on the wooden surface, his
mouth half-open, lip trembling under his moustache ✖ ✖ I left my backpack on the floor
and walked over in silence. I gave him a kiss on the
cheek and stood expectantly. From the kitchen there
came a familiar whistle. Through the open door I
saw a hand holding a mug, then an old shoe, and
finally the rest of tío Aarón: his T-shirt all grubby
and ripped at the collar, the back of his neck red and

peeling. He offered a smile, though he didn't dare hug me. Papá looked at me and said, dryly, pressing his lips together: I've been laid off ✖ My tío would tell me later that he'd gone to see his brother at the accountant's office. I thought: That wretch is gonna bring the whole family down, he's a leech, disgracing everyone around him. But I was wrong: Aarón had rescued his brother, who when he arrived was already wandering through the aisles of toys, lost to himself, chewing over the news ✖

✖   ✖   ✖

So what do we do now? I asked him that night, as I was dozing off next to him on the bed. Tomorrow I'll look for another job, he replied ✖ ✖ ✖

✖ I was left listening to his snores. Beneath them, fear of dark corners with their spiders and muffled roars that possess you like an electric shock from the ankles to the top of your head and, embracing you, whisper:

We will never leave you ✖

Never ✖

Your father will die, will crumble into ash, and you will wander through the desert like a wound turned into a flower ✖

And so it was ✖   ✖   ✖   ✖   ✖

I understood that part of papá santo's anxiety was down to the fact our savings were slowly running out ✖ There were no more gringos to go to for handouts ✖ I'd get home from school, see papá santo and my tío, and the two of them would smile, barely registering my presence ✖ ✖ ✖ ✖ ✖ ✖ ✖ ✖ ✖ ✖ ✖ ✖ ✖ ✖ ✖ ✖ They showed me their teeth in an expression that tried to be reassuring ✖ ✖ I said hello, hiding my sadness, and went up to lie on the bed: giving myself over to the physical activity of enduring the heat, and nothing else ✖ ✖ ✖ ✖ Hunger ✖ ✖ ✖ ✖ Sometimes, in my lowest moments, I managed to swallow my pride and be nice at school ✖ ✖ Over the course of a break, maybe two or even three, I'd talk nonstop to girls in my class whom I'd never spoken to before ✖ ✖ ✖ All so someone would invite me over for an after-school snack ✖ Anything for a piece of bread and jam and a cup of tea ✖ ✖ ✖ ✖ ✖ ✖ Or else I'd go down to the sea and sit there watching the dogs ✖ ✖ ✖ They used to run around near the water and bark at the seagulls, who would respond by circling above them, laughing madly ✖ ✖ ✖ When the sun started to set, a sort of peace would settle over the coastline, and some of the dogs would come over to me, wet, tongues lolling, kindly and curious ✖ ✖ ✖ ✖ ✖ ✖ ✖ I'd talk to them about Pato, letting threads of sand trickle out from closed fists onto my legs ✖ ✖

✖ ✖ ✖ ✖ ✖ ✖ ✖ ✖ ✖ ✖ ✖ ✖ ✖ ✖ ✖ ✖ ✖ ✖

✖ ✖ ✖ ✖ ✖ ✖ ✖ ✖ ✖ ✖ ✖ ✖ ✖ ✖ ✖ ✖ ✖
✖ ✖ ✖ ✖ ✖ ✖ ✖ ✖ ✖ ✖ ✖ ✖

I thought the year would see itself out according to that unbearable routine ✖ ✖ ✖

✖ ✖ ✖ But in the last week of classes Sandra's little sister came up to me during a break and whispered in my ear:

Your papá's a queer.

She went off with her friends and left me there ✖ ✖ From then on I decided to watch him on my days off ✖ It didn't take long before Sandra's sister's comment began to make sense ✖ ✖ His behavior had become suspicious: some week nights papá went out and didn't come back until late ✖ ✖ ✖ ✖ ✖ At first I thought he was just going down to the living room to think, but one day I decided to pretend I was asleep and wait to see what was really going on ✖ ✖ ✖ When I went down no one was there ✖ Another night I followed him, carefully ✖ He went to a place I'd spent my whole childhood believing to be bad, very bad ✖ The adults used to tell us: Don't go anywhere near Los Troncos, that club's a den of iniquity. Nobody there has a soul. They've all lost their way. But that's where he was. He went in. I couldn't believe it ✖ I jumped up onto the wall and climbed down the other side using some crates piled up in the courtyard ✖ I stuck my head around a door and walked down a corridor ✖ Stood spying for a little while and then spotted him: among the miners who'd just gotten paid, a few lively transvestites, and some Colombian whores, papá santo was thinking ✖ Leaning on the bar with a beaded pint of beer, papá santo was thinking ✖ ✖ I followed him a couple more times, and the scene was always the same. I came to think that in truth papá santo wasn't a queer, as Sandra's sister had said, but that he simply needed company, noise, to feel the presence of bodies and smells while he sipped a cold drink ✖ ✖ And though most of the time they played rancheras, Sound, or strident cumbia, I noticed that occasionally someone would request a Peruvian waltz, or something even sadder. Then everyone seemed to come together in a gesture of collective intimacy, as though arm in arm they could repair the pieces of a shattered soul. All the queens, the whores, and the rest of the customers would listen to those sad songs together, like the ones Isidora and I listen to now, on days when we're feeling particularly listless ✖

Jesus answered, Verily, verily, I say unto thee, Except a man be born of water and of the Spirit, he cannot enter into the kingdom of God.

John 3:5

Perhaps to save him from himself, after I followed him one last time I said to papá santo:

I'm ready ✖

✖ He understood and hugged me ✖

I went Tuesday and Thursday afternoons to the Latter Day Saints school, to prepare myself for becoming a Saint ✖ The old man seemed to regain some interest in life now that he had to guide his daughter along the paths of God ✖ ✖ ✖ ✖

✖ ✖ In the meantime we traveled to Fray Santiago, an abandoned salt-mining town where my great-grandfather had lived. Right out in the sticks, just past the synthetic saltpeter ✖ ✖ ✖ His son had left as soon as he could. Papá santo never spoke of his own father, maybe out of shame. But that day he took me in the pickup to look for his bones ✖ Crouching in the shade against a wall, two llama herders were chewing coca ✖ In the distance, up on the mountain range, a dozen motorcyclists sliced down the flanks of earth and hawthorn ✖ ✖ ✖ ✖ ✖ ✖ ✖

A kilometer from the salt-mining town there was a field of crosses, most wooden, some iron. We stopped in front of one. Papá santo lit a cigarette, rolled up his shirtsleeves, and went back to the pickup for a spade ✖ He dug until I could barely see his head.

Just as dusk was setting in, he emerged with some stiff, dusty pants, a pair of worn shoes, some bones, and a ring ✖ ✖ We sold the ring and planned to live a couple of months longer on the proceeds ✖ The clothes we left lying on the patio behind the house ✖ The bones we took to the temple of the Latter Day Saints ✖ Papá said we had to baptize our ancestors in order to win favor from heaven and make sure their souls would rest in peace ✖

Don't you think it's unfair, hija, that just because he didn't know the word of the Prophet the old man will never get his own little corner of heaven?

I gave him a disconcerted look but managed not to contradict him ✖ ✖ ✖ So as soon as you've been baptized we'll arrange this next one, that way

we'll close the circle, our salvation will be assured
✖ What about Pato? ✖ ✖ ✖
✖ ✖ ✖ ✖ ✖ ✖ ✖ ✖ ✖ ✖ ✖ ✖ ✖ ✖
What about him?
✖ ✖
✖ ✖ ✖ ✖ ✖ ✖
Aren't we going to baptize Pato too?
✖ ✖ ✖ ✖ ✖ ✖ ✖
No. Not him.
✖ ✖
When we got back the llama herders had gone
✖ ✖ ✖ ✖ ✖ ✖ ✖ ✖ ✖ ✖ ✖ ✖ ✖ ✖ ✖ ✖ ✖ ✖
✖ ✖ ✖ ✖ ✖ ✖ ✖ ✖ ✖ ✖ ✖ ✖ ✖ ✖ ✖ ✖ ✖ ✖
✖ ✖ ✖ In the afternoon I walked through
Fray Santiago. I was as tired then as I am now that
I'm dying, maybe even more ✖ ✖ ✖ ✖
✖ That tiredness that huddles down at the back of
your neck and never lets you go. The same tiredness
that meant Tim ended up inside a bunch of cans,
at one with the tuna out at sea ✖ ✖ ✖ ✖
✖ The same tiredness that smashed my bones to
pieces the day I submerged myself in the pool at
the temple: there were three of us, a well-groomed
young man called Brother Jaime, Sister Ruth, and
me. All dressed in white ✖ ✖ The room was underneath the temple. Brother Jaime led me by the hand
toward the pool ✖ We went in up to our waists.
The cold paralyzed my groin and I felt a sinister
tingling ✖ I thought: It's Jehovah, punishing me
for screwing Jesulé and for my escapades at Playa
Roja ✖ ✖ ✖ For hanging out with fornicators and

other bad sorts. For allowing myself to be baptized an unbeliever ✖ ✖

✖ They submerged me three times, blessing me on each occasion

in the name of the Father,
the Son,
and the Holy Ghost

and I saw how my words came out false ✖ I was spitting ashes ✖ ✖ I sank into the water, face up, the nape of my neck held in Brother Jaime's open palm ✖   ✖   ✖   ✖ Papá santo could not have been happier, and in my room a white dress that Ruth had lent me was waiting on the bed ✖✖✖✖✖ He'd organized a meal, and the Brothers Bryan and Josías, Sister Ruth, Brother Jaime, my tío Aarón, and some other Mormons I didn't know were downstairs ✖ There was baked fish and chips ✖ ✖ They looked happy ✖ Before eating we held hands and Brother Jaime blessed the table. Blessed everyone present. And the day's witnesses. And the doorway that had opened up for Sister Nancy. He took the opportunity to remind us of the virtue of restraint, the importance of holding firm against temptation. The cunning serpent lies in wait for the weak of spirit ✖ We gave thanks. I ate fries with my fingers and we all drank lemonade ✖ Then tío Aarón told a story about how, twenty years ago in the south, he'd had to help some farm

workers hunt a huge snake ✖ It had been killing the
hens ✖ He grabbed a kerosene lamp and headed
out in search of it with a group of men and dogs ✖
Although the problem wasn't the hens, he explained
✖ The owner had plenty of them, and it wasn't like
he was so short of money that he'd miss just one or
two ✖ The problem was that the snake wasn't just
any snake, it was one of those clever ones, the ones
that eat and eat and grow every year, not only getting longer but also fatter, growing rings like trees,
and getting savvier too ✖ Eventually the only thing
that can satiate them is a woman's milk ✖ ✖ ✖ ✖
Around there they used to say there were a number of demonic snakes, slaves to an unquenchable
thirst, that could sneak into houses, slither along the
pipes, and enter women's bedrooms ✖ There they'd
quietly settle at their breasts and suckle ✖   ✖   ✖
After a few days the women would die in a delirium,
their breasts like dried figs ✖   It looked like the
owner's wife had died from one such snake, so there
was nothing to be done but go and hunt it down. It
was known that breast milk left the snakes drunk,
and often you'd find them lying by the side of the
path or tangled somewhere near the house, sleeping
✖ We returned from the raid empty-handed, and
one man down ✖   ✖   ✖   ✖   ✖ Juan García
had just vanished ✖   We didn't go out again after
that ✖

✖ The Mormon Brothers cleared their throats awk-
wardly. Jaime interrupted the story with a question

about the day's baptism ✖ ✖   The rest I already knew: Juan García and the owner's wife were lovers. The snake never existed. García was found three weeks later. His body had been shredded in an irrigation canal ✖ There was nothing for tío Aarón to do except carry on eating ✖ ✖

    ✖   ✖
    ✖   ✖   ✖

Let him kiss me with the kisses of his mouth: for thy love is better than wine. Because of the savor of thy good ointments thy name is as ointment poured forth, therefore do the virgins love thee. Draw me, we will run after thee: the king hath brought me into his chambers: we will be glad and rejoice in thee, we will remember thy love more than wine: the upright love thee.

Song of Songs 1:2–4

A couple of days after my baptism I got home from school and tío Aarón wasn't there ✖ ✖ ✖ The next morning I asked papá if he knew why my tío hadn't come back the night before ✖ ✖ ✖ Your tío won't be coming back at all, he replied ✖ ✖ How come? Did you throw him out? ✖

✖ It's the only way to make him see that in life you've got to keep your head above water ✖ Stay sober, hardworking, devout ✖ ✖ ✖ You can't just give up ✖ ✖ ✖ That was the end of the conversation ✖ I never saw him again, and to this day I think it was the Latter Day Saints Brothers that led to their falling out

✖ I loved him, despite the smell, and his lack of composure, and his feigned happiness ✖ ✖ ✖ ✖

✖ ✖ Papá santo didn't even bother to explain it to me. He seemed happier talking to himself, alone in the courtyard or the bathroom ✖ ✖ ✖ ✖ ✖ ✖ ✖ Muttering to himself ✖ The money from the ring ran out. The two of us lived in daily uncertainty ✖ ✖ ✖ Papá stopped going to Los Troncos ✖ He spent a whole day in the back courtyard organizing the boxes ✖ When he finished he sat down to sunbathe and pretty much just stayed there ✖ ✖ A month later he was black ✖ He'd say: The Bible inside, the sun outside, and would laugh ✖ I'd look at him, then go back to my homework ✖ At school I stole bread from the cafeteria ✖ ✖ ✖ I went to doctors' offices too and out of sheer pity they gave me powdered milk ✖ I'd walk along the beach and eat it by the spoonful ✖ But once they got to know me they'd stop letting me have it, so one day I walked to the only one I hadn't been to yet, on the outskirts of Ch, in a slum called El Cobre ✖ The sun was setting and the buzzards were bidding it farewell, gliding between the sea and the mountains ✖ ✖ ✖ ✖ ✖ ✖ ✖ Seagulls, dogs, pelicans, even a group of children were feasting in the dumps and landfill sites surrounding the slums ✖ At the end of an alleyway named Syria Passage, in the loneliest corner in all of Ch, behind a car, there was an empty lot ✖ ✖ ✖ ✖ ✖ ✖ ✖ ✖ ✖ ✖ I came out of the doctor's office, lifted my eyes from the bag of powdered milk, and spotted the Mormon Brothers swaying sweatily as they walked

✖ They went around a corner, down the alleyway to the empty plot of land ✖ ✖ ✖ I followed and, peering through some planks of wood, on my knees, saw them ✖

After thousands of kilometers on foot and two years of missionary work going from house to house, it was there, against the wall, as the sun was setting on the hottest day of the year, that Brother Bryan kissed Brother Josías for the first time ✖ They devoured each other for two minutes and then stood staring, awkward, each one searching for something in the other's face ✖

✖ ✖ ✖ ✖ ✖ ✖

✖ ✖ ✖ ✖ ✖ ✖ ✖ ✖ ✖ Three days later they turned up at the house ✖ They looked uneasy ✖ I opened the door, let them in, and went up to my room. I couldn't look them in the face ✖ That night I asked papá why they'd come ✖

✖ ✖ They offered me a job as a gardener at the temple ✖ And? ✖ And nothing, I'm an accountant, not a gardener ✖ But what are we going to eat? ✖ Powdered milk. But if you like tomorrow we'll go to La Gallineta, they're bound to give us something on credit ✖ ✖ ✖ ✖

I had my ear pressed against his back and heard everything as though from the bottom of the municipal swimming pool ✖   ✖   ✖ I went to sleep happy at the prospect ✖ ✖

He showed up at school at lunchtime. I went to wash up in the bathroom, rinse my mouth out, brush my hair, prepare myself for a delicious meal, a real one, for the first time in a month ✖ ✖ ✖

But they wouldn't give us any credit at all ✖

✖ ✖ ✖ ✖ ✖ ✖ ✖ ✖ ✖ ✖ ✖ ✖ ✖ ✖
✖ ✖ ✖ ✖ ✖ ✖ ✖ ✖ ✖ ✖ ✖ ✖ ✖ ✖ ✖
✖ ✖ ✖ ✖ ✖ ✖ ✖ ✖
✖ ✖
✖ ✖ ✖ ✖ ✖ ✖ ✖ ✖ ✖ ✖
✖ ✖ ✖ ✖ ✖ ✖ ✖ ✖
✖ ✖ ✖ ✖
✖ ✖ ✖ ✖ ✖ ✖ ✖ ✖ ✖ ✖ ✖ ✖ ✖ ✖ ✖ ✖
✖ ✖ ✖ ✖ ✖ ✖
✖ ✖ ✖ ✖ ✖ ✖ ✖ ✖

We wandered aimlessly through Ch until a car horn jolted us out of our daydream ✖ On the corner, the gringos' driver, that pale, thin Chilean, was signaling to me ✖ Papá santo shouted at him: What do you want with my daughter ✖ Nothing, Pastor, never mind ✖ The driver looked at me, lifted his eyebrows, realizing he might have fucked up ✖ He took a piece of paper out of his pocket, dropped it on the ground, and left ✖ ✖ ✖ I ran to pick up the piece of paper. There was a phone number on it ✖ ✖ Some guy from Ch who was traveling the world as a kind of guru had decided to make a film based on his autobiographical novel ✖ ✖ The voice on the other end of the line explained to me that they needed extras, a lot of extras, and that even though they'd brought people in from elsewhere they could definitely add another gentleman and a girl to the crowd ✘ ✘ ✘ Bring old clothes if you've got any, he said. I'm Rubén, you'll find us just off the Panamerican Highway, twenty kilometers after the turnoff for the Pobre canal ✘ ✘ ✘ ✘ ✘ There's a whole miniature town, you can't miss us ✘ ✘ ✘ Papá shook out some of his grandfather's old clothes and his mother's first communion dress and off we went ✘ ✘ ✘ ✘ The fake town was the guru's idea of what Ch had been like in his childhood: newly painted houses, people dressed up in traditional pampas outfits, and dogs and kids jumping around together ✘ On one side of the miniature town: the long silhouettes of the Romany hanging out with the production team ✘

✘ Among their copper faces, wandering around with a smile behind his cigarette, Jesulé ✘ ✘ ✘ ✘ ✘ ✘
✘ ✘
✘ ✘

✘ ✘ ✘ ✘ ✘ ✘ ✘ ✘ ✘ ✘ ✘ ✘ ✘ ✘ ✘ ✘ ✘
✘ ✘ ✘ ✘ ✘ ✘ ✘ ✘ ✘ ✘ ✘ ✘ ✘ ✘ ✘ ✘ ✘

(MORPHINE: 10MG I.M./S.C 6–8 HRS; 30MG PO 6–8 HRS. CODEINE: 30–60MG PO 6–8 HRS)
✘ ✘

✖ ✖ ✖ ✖ ✖ ✖

Everyone's gotta die of something, I tell Isidorita as I ask her to increase the dose with the sweetest smile I can muster

✖✖✖✖✖✖✖✖✖✖✖✖✖✖✖✖✖✖✖✖✖✖
✖✖✖✖✖✖✖✖✖✖✖✖✖✖✖✖✖✖

✖ ✖ And so acting saved us for a while. We went back and forth from the miniature town for a month and a half ✖ Sometimes we went in the car, but mostly we took the shuttle bus from the town square ✖

There were glorious days when all we had to do was walk through the streets with the rest of the crowd with no apparent purpose, even when the camera was nowhere to be seen. The guru would stand on a box and issue vague instructions through a loud-speaker: This is really happening, don't think about the film, just tune into what the earth is saying to you. At first we just stood there, our legs stretched out for the next step, not knowing what he meant by listening to the earth ✖ Other days we all had to repeat the same scene over and over again, up to fifteen times, because of something to do with the light, and because the guru wasn't entirely convinced by something or other ✖

In all that coming and going, I started feeling Jesulé's eyes on me again ✖ ✖ ✖

I pretended to be oblivious. I clung to papá santo, who'd be dressed as an office worker from the salt-mining town, or as a grocer, and we'd wander with the rest of the extras, sunk in an eternal Sunday. There were hours spent just looking, mainly at faces, though also, often, at my feet, at the dress I moved inside: covered in lace and pleats and embroidered with false pearls ✖ ✖ The tangle of footprints braided in the dust ✖ ✖ ✖ ✖ ✖ The rust and the salt ✖ Bodies in the sun or the shade ✖ ✖ ✖ Irritating children ✖ ✖ Women, walking tirelessly, gossiping, all sassy in their little groups ✖

One evening the buses arrived to take us back to Ch, but with night setting in and everyone already on board, none of them was able to start ✖ The production team decided all they could do was accept the situation and get on with it. Apologize, hand out coffee and snacks ✖ ✖ ✖ ✖ ✖ I leaned against the window and was out like a light. At some point in the early morning my papá crossed the aisle of exhausted faces and got out ✖ I saw him light a cigarette and disappear into the desert ✖ ✖ ✖ ✖ After a while I also got off the bus and walked over to the Romany camp ✖ ✖ ✖ ✖ ✖ In a clearing surrounded by tents, about twenty people were watching the fire and heating up bits of metal ✖ And there was Jesulé ✖ ✖ ✖ I stood there watching him, and at some point we exchanged looks.

He came over quietly, took me by the hand, and we talked, sitting on our haunches near the bonfire. He offered me his jacket ✖   ✖   You're shivering in that thin dress, kid, he said ✖ I asked him what they were up to ✖ He gestured to a group of Romany gathered around a wheel: Retreading a tire ✖ They were cutting into the rubber with hot nails ✖ Best bet's to sell 'em in Bolivia, no question. More money, less paperwork ✖ I nodded and rubbed my cold hands ✖ A while later we went into a tent. We fucked and then he lay down next to me, serious, looking at the canvas ceiling ✖

Best you go and sleep, kid ✖

I walked quickly back to the bus ✖ Papá wasn't there, and I wouldn't see him until early afternoon the next day ✖ In the morning I went back to where the Romany were. Jesulé was smiling, shirtless, his face in the sun ✖   We did it again in the same place ✖ When he pulled out his penis it was all covered in a blood I'd never seen before ✖ ✖ My period had come for the first time, three or four years after all the women I knew, and I didn't know what to do ✖ ✖   ✖   ✖   Jesulé felt and smelled his fingers, more brown than red. He gave me a startled look and quickly pulled up his pants ✖ You could get pregnant now, paisa, he said. And it's best we do this some other time ✖ I stood up, burning with shame. Imperial maps blossomed on sections of my dress. I ran in silence to the bus ✖ ✖ ✖ I could feel the laughter behind me ✖ ✖ My ears and my face were ringing ✖ ✖ ✖ ✖ On the bus people were already waking up, and as soon as they saw me, legs held wide, threads of blood dripping down my calves, they called one of the female technicians ✖ ✖ ✖ ✖ ✖ ✖ ✖ ✖ ✖ ✖ ✖ ✖ ✖

They took me to a cabin, offered me use of the toilet, sanitary pads, and clean clothes ✖ ✖ ✖ ✖ ✖ Papá santo, naturally, had no idea about any of this ✖ He didn't even ask what had happened when I found him again among the crowd, dressed up like a mayor ✖ ✖ ✖ He just materialized from among the surge of extras, twizzling his walking stick in the air. He offered me his arm and we went on with our eternal wandering like it was nothing at all ✖ ✖ ✖ ✖ Behind him, among lights, cables, and pulleys, my grandmother's communion dress hung out to dry ✖

✖ ✖ ✖ ✖ As soon as I arrived on set Jesulé disappeared as fast as he'd shown up, and though the Romany stayed where they were I didn't feel him looking as he did his rounds again ✖ ✖ It was like his eyes had dried up ✖ ✖ I thought I'd earned myself a Romany curse ✖

I felt like a pillar of salt, burned inside, a bitch struck down by ringworm ✖ ✖ ✖

The next night, back at home now, papá santo repeated his little performance. I'm going for a walk, won't be long, he said after dinner, and didn't come back till early morning ✗ I was distracted trying not to let my period stain my clothes, changing my sanitary pad as often as I could ✗ ✗ ✗ I watched worriedly as the blood kept coming, bit by bit ✗ ✗ ✗ ✗ Three days, four ✗ ✗ ✗ ✗ ✗ I would have died of shame if I'd had to ask the recording assistants for more pads ✗ ✗ ✗ ✗ What on earth would they think of a girl who bleeds as much as this? How many days does a period last? ✗

✗ ✗ ✗ ✗ Two days later papá got into the car, fled the miniature town without me, and didn't come back ✗ ✗ ✗ ✗ ✗ I'd gone to the bathroom and by the time I came out he'd vanished into thin air.

✗ ✗ ✗ ✗ ✗ ✗ ✗ ✗ ✗✗ ✗ ✗ ✗ ✗

✗ ✗ ✗ ✗ ✗ ✗ ✗ ✗ ✗ ✗ ✗ ✗ ✗ ✗ ✗ ✗ ✗ ✗ ✗ At the end of the day, when I realized I was on my own, I went over to one of the technicians and asked them what to do. She replied that I could easily take the bus, like I'd sometimes done before with papá perdido, my lost father. But then what? I decided to swallow my shame and get on the bus as though it was perfectly normal to do so by myself. I leaned against the window in the back row and squeezed my knees together, waiting for my anxiety to pass ✘ ✘ ✘ ✘   When I got home the car was parked outside ✘ ✘ ✘ But there was no sign of papá ✘

✘ That night I couldn't sleep. I wrapped both arms and legs around a long pillow. Waited in the dark, sleepless. Not sure if my eyes were open or closed: an uneasy calm ✘ ✘ ✘ ✘ ✘ ✘ ✘ I decided not to go back to the film set. I preferred to go hungry in Ch and be in the house, to get home from school, dump my backpack, shower, and go walking on the beach, instead of spending all day mixed up in the traffic of people rehearsing ✘ The heat there was unbearable. Everyone's faces, except the guru's, swelled up with the days, the clipped instructions, the dead time. At least in the house it was quiet, peaceful I shivered on the floor, my back freezing against the tiles, thinking about papá perdido ✘ Whiled away the hours to the sound of the TV; I imagined Jesulé looking at the scene like a boy looks at a cage of monkeys. Hands in his own pockets, mind on other people's ✘ Because although there was good money to be had, plenty of it, you really had to want it ✘ And for the guru coins were just flies to be slapped away: another problem to avoid, like his assistants or technicians ✘ ✘ ✘ ✘ ✘ ✘   ✘   ✘   ✘ It was interesting to watch him on those eternal days filming a single scene. His gestures. He stood with one hand covering his mouth, his eyes bright, unblinking, and his reaction was as arbitrary as it was awful: he'd look at the assistants and wait for their opinion in order to laugh in their faces. Sometimes he'd shout Cut! before the actors had even appeared, and he used to walk around in circles, indignant, ignoring the murmured advice of his lackeys ✖ ✖ ✖ Tim would tell me, a while later, that the two film crews had met one day because the guru was interested in using some panoramic shots they'd taken of the countryside. So there they were, the two crews, eating their ceviche, glaring stiffly at each other. Naturally the guru didn't eat anything. He neither ate nor drank. Sometimes he didn't even breathe. He'd watch suspiciously and intervene with some comment calculated to make everyone uncomfortable. Thank God there was a lot of wine, Tim told me, and before the situation got out of hand his team was drunk enough to quietly retreat. The lead actor, who they all feared would cause some scandal, didn't get worked up at all ✖ ✖ ✖ ✖ ✖ ✖ ✖ He raised toast after toast and then left, as agreed, with the rest of the crew, without causing any trouble ✖ ✖ ✖ ✖ ✖ ✖ ✖ ✖ ✖ But the guru didn't matter anymore, nor did papá perdido ✖ ✖ ✖ I felt like I had to worry about myself ✖ ✖ ✖ I only went one more time to the miniature town, a week later ✖ ✖ ✖ ✖ ✖ ✖ I spotted Jesulé as soon as I arrived ✖ ✖ ✖ ✖ I went over, not taking my eyes off him, and said in a quiet voice: Buy the car off me

✖ He nodded ✖ ✖ Told me I should go home as soon as the buses started leaving and he'd be along in a little while ✖ ✖ ✖ ✖ ✖ Night came ✖ ✖ He arrived in a pickup with three other paisanos. I invited them in, they drank some water, and put five hundred lucas down on the table ✖ I took it and gave them the keys ✖ ✖ ✖ ✖ ✖ ✖ ✖ ✖ And the Pastor? the Romany asked me at some point ✖ ✖ ✖ The Pastor's lost in the mountains and his sheep have nowhere to graze, I answered ✖ ✖ ✖ ✖ He threw me an Ah, held out his hand, then left ✖ ✖ ✖ ✖ ✖ ✖ ✖ ✖ ✖ ✖ ✖ ✖ ✖ ✖ ✖ ✖

✖ ✖ As soon as it landed on the table all I could think about was the wad of notes ✖ ✖ About what I was going to spend it on ✖ ✖ ✖ I went out at once for chicken and fries and a Coke ✖ ✖ ✖ ✖ ✖ Fell asleep on the table, my fingers smeared with grease, breathing heavily, laughing to myself, looking at the chicken bones scattered on the tray ✖ ✖

✖ ✖ ✖ ✖ ✖ The next day I ate two italianos and a chacarero. In the afternoon I bought a new phone, pearl earrings, jeans, and shoes ✖ Walked through Ch swinging the bags ✖ ✖ Feeling their weight ✖ Happy ✖ ✖ ✖ ✖ ✖

✖ ✖ In the evening I found myself behind the Brothers again. Practically the same place as before ✖ ✖ I followed them to the same vacant lot ✖ ✖ ✖ ✖ This time I managed to film them on my phone ✘ ✘ ✘ ✘ ✘ ✘ ✘ ✘ ✘ ✘ The next day I woke up very early, ran to the town square, and waited till they showed up ✘ ✘   ✘ ✘ They walked quietly, still half asleep, necks exposed to the sun ✘ ✘ ✘ ✘ ✘ ✘ This time there was no furtive kiss. Rather, they went to the bus station. We waited there forty minutes, them sitting reading or talking, drinking bottled water, while I hid cramped behind a kiosk ✘ Then a bright pink-and-black bus appeared ✘ ✘ ✘ ✘ ✘ ✘ ✘ ✘ ✘ I waited for the Brothers to board, then asked one of the old parking guys where the bus was going and when the next one would be ✘ Cajón Colgado, he said, and you'll have to wait till tomorrow, there's only one a day ✘ ✘ ✘

✘ ✘ ✘

I went back the next morning and waited for the scene to repeat itself ✘ I jumped on board just as the bus was about to leave. They were sitting at the back, and didn't notice me ✘ ✘ ✘ ✘ ✘ As I looked out at the landscape I thought about papá perdido ✘ ✘ ✘ ✘ Imagined him by his old man's grave, watering the cans of plastic flowers, doodling in the dirt, feeling his way along the walls, chasing echoes ✘ ✘ ✘ ✘ ✘ I thought the journey would be a lot quicker ✘ It was almost midday before we were stopped by a police car ✘ The bus driver looked back and said: Anyone going further is gonna have to walk, this is as far as I can take you ✘ ✘ ✘ ✘ I covered my face with my jacket and waited till everyone else had gotten off. The driver's hand on my knee alerted me ✖ ✖ The other passengers were already on their way, scattered. Some with luggage, others with children ✖ ✖ ✖ ✖

✖ ✖ ✖ The cops explained that they'd stopped the traffic because of the festival. I walked slowly, hoping nothing would make the Brothers turn around ✖

✖ The cops didn't say so but it was common knowledge that during the festival of the virgin everyone in L.L would get wasted half-secretly and then go out into the streets and knock each other around ✖ Every once in a while somebody actually died ✖ ✖ In any case, the whole thing went on for three days and, what with so much apparent lawlessness, the police were out in force, waiting quietly on the road five kilometers from the church.

✖ ✖

Sometimes, out of boredom, they'd have a drink or two themselves, despite the supposed dry law

✖ ✖ ✖ ✖ ✖ ✖ ✖ ✖
✖ ✖

✖ ✖ ✖ ✖ ✖ ✖ ✖ ✖ ✖ ✖ ✖ ✖ ✖ ✖ ✖
✖ ✖ ✖ ✖ ✖ ✖ ✖ ✖ ✖ ✖

Virgencita of Good Death, a collective epiphany in LL
[And the virgin, doctor? Can you see the virgin?]

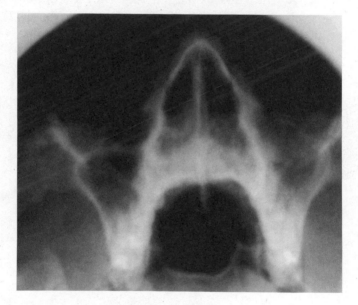

921

× × × × × × × × × × × × × × × × × ×
× × × × × × × × × × × × × × × × × ×
× × × × × × × × × ×

Never have you refused
help to those in need;
they have found peace and joy
in your loving embrace:
the wrongdoer turns to you
in hours of fear:
show us, merciful Mother,
the kindness of your love
IX, Prayer to Our Lady of the Good Death

And how did they choose their carnival queen? asks Isidora when I tell her about anything to do with those northern towns ✖ ✖ ✖ ✖ Not all of them have carnivals, I reply ✖ ✖ ✖ And obviously none of them come close to the one in the big port ✖ ✖ That festival in LL was in devotion to the local virgencita, that's all ✖ ✖ People give offerings ✖ ✖ Make the long yearly pilgrimage to a spot in the middle of nowhere and say to her: Here I am again ✖

✖ ✖ ✖ ✖ ✖ ✖ ✖ ✖ Before the time I followed the Brothers all I knew about LL was hearsay ✖ ✖ It was only a little festival but it involved a couple of bands you used to find doing the rounds in the north that time of year, ones that used to pass through Ch as well ✖ ✖ It's not that they didn't have a queen, I explained to Isidora, who was visibly unsettled by the idea, rather that the queen is the Virgin ✖ ✖ She looked at me suspiciously and muttered: Well what's the point of the carnival then? No alliances, no competition, no new candidates ✖ ✖ ✖ ✖ ✖ It's about devotion, I insisted ✖

✖ ✖ I arrived on the second day, so the official processions had already passed through. Most people had left, and there didn't seem to be any commotion coming from the first adobe houses that emerged in the distance ✖ ✖ ✖ ✖ I waited for the Brothers to disappear into the village, sitting by a couple of pickups carrying the last few festival-goers. Some of them, the more pious ones perhaps, had brought saint's cards, prayers for safe travel, calendars, plaster statues of the Virgin in different sizes. The rest also brought mobile phones, toys, American clothes, deodorant, underwear ✖ ✖ ✖ ✖

✖ ✖ ✖ ✖ When the sun started to set and the road was empty, I walked ✖ ✖ ✖ ✖ ✖ In the square a handful of old men and women surrounded a bigger handful of musicians, dressed up to the nines in red and white. Among the crowds, calm, solid faces flashed and vanished in the light from the bonfires ✖ ✖ ✖ ✖ The trumpets hanging, the tubas crouching, the bass drums lying down ✖ ✖

✖ ✖ ✖ ✖ ✖ ✖ ✖ ✖ ✖ ✖ ✖ ✖ ✖ ✖ ✖ ✖
✖ ✖ ✖ I was breathless, still, as the others were
still ✖ ✖ ✖ ✖ ✖ and I entered into the silence ✖
✖ ✖ ✖ ✖ ✖ ✖ ✖ ✖ ✖ ✖ ✖ ✖ ✖ ✖ ✖ ✖
✖ ✖ ✖ ✖ ✖ ✖ ✖ ✖ ✖ ✖ ✖ ✖ ✖ ✖ ✖ ✖
✖ ✖ ✖ ✖ ✖ ✖ ✖ ✖ ✖ ✖ ✖ ✖ ✖ ✖ ✖ ✖
✖ ✖ ✖ ✖ ✖ ✖ ✖ ✖ ✖ ✖ ✖ ✖ ✖ ✖ ✖ ✖
✖ ✖ ✖ ✖ ✖ ✖ ✖ ✖ ✖ ✖ ✖ ✖ ✖ ✖ ✖ ✖

First, there was a low murmur in the square, drawn
out and sustained by the sun that was plunging
toward the horizon. Then a boy who was struggling
to reach around a bass drum gave the signal. He
lifted his arm and the band sliced through the
pampa with their grand finale ✖ ✖ I felt like
I'd just had my ears cleaned ✖ ✖ ✖ Something
whipped across my back and suddenly I was the
only one who wasn't moving ✖ The stampedes
of elephants descending from the skirts of la
virgencita resounded inside our heads. Andean
trunks swaying frenetically ✖ ✖ ✖ Dust rising as
though the sheer strength of people's faith might
transform it into a hurricane, with me in its eye, in
its center. And just like that, like a claw emerging
from a wall of wind and earth, within five minutes
they were squeezing my collarbone ✖ Behind me,
Bryan and Josías, smiling, rosy like pigs, drenched
in sweat ✖

The three of us, serene, looked at each other ✖

Everyone else vibrated, and there we stood.

✖   What are you doing here, Sister Nancy, shouted Josías ✖ I smiled and shrugged. I was bored, I answered, glad to be able to shout back ✖ ✖ ✖ People's silhouettes grew longer, and suddenly I couldn't even really see the Brothers ✖ ✖ As the drums sounded my knees buckled ✖ ✖ And I fell ✖

✖ ✖ ✖ ✖ ✖ ✖ ✖ ✖ ✖ ✖ ✖ ✖ ✖ ✖ ✖

I woke up on a sofa in a white room. Sitting next to a window, her elbow on the table, an indigenous Mormon woman was reading quietly ✖ ✖ ✖ ✖ I tried to sit up, asking after Bryan and Josías ✖ She raised her head, gave me a smile that reached her eyes, and said: We'd better head to the dining room, Sister, so you don't faint on us again ✖ ✖ ✖ In the next room fifteen uniformed Saints were eating, all of them young. The place was narrow and white: bare walls, two doors, plastic chairs and tablecloths ✖ ✖ ✖ They smiled at me but I felt cold. I decided to concentrate on the bread and broth. Not even the woman who'd been looking after me met my eyes again. The windows shivered with the noise coming from the plaza ✖ ✖ ✖ Where were the lovebirds? ✖ ✖ God only knows what they were up to ✖ ✖ ✖ ✖ ✖ ✖ A wave of tiredness was washing over me and the soup was never-ending

And the steam blurring my vision

And my nose starting to run   ✘

✘ They were already starting to laugh at my nodding head when a car horn sounded over all the trumpeting ✘ I thought no one had heard it. I was the only one who turned to look ✘ ✘ ✘ ✘ Through one of the doors Bryan was gesturing at me to hurry ✘ ✘ ✘ ✘ We got into a van and set off back to Ch ✘ ✘ ✘ ✘ ✘ ✘ ✘ ✘ ✘ ✘ ✘ ✘ ✘ ✘ ✘
✘ ✘ ✘ ✘ ✘ ✘ ✘ ✘ ✘ ✘ ✘ ✘ ✘ ✘ ✘ ✘ ✘
✘ ✘ ✘ ✘ ✘ ✘ ✘ ✘ ✘ ✘ ✘ ✘ ✘ ✘ ✘ ✘ ✘
✘ ✘ ✘ ✘ ✘ ✘ ✘ ✘ ✘ ✘ ✘ ✘ ✘ ✘ ✘ ✘ ✘
✘ ✘
✘
✘ ✘ ✘ ✘
✘

✘ ✘ ✘ ✘ ✘ ✘ ✘ ✘ ✘ ✘ ✘
✘ ✘ ✘ ✘ ✘ ✘ ✘ ✘ ✘

We're worried about you, Sister Nancy: you can't just go through life all by yourself, the Saints told me outside my house. Elder Jaime waited at the wheel with the engine running. He hadn't spoken the whole way back to Ch, his brow severe and lips a thin line. The lights in the living room and upstairs were still off. Ashamed of not knowing where papá santo was, I knew I had to keep them talking till they decided to go ✘ ✘ I leaned closer to the Brothers and said quietly: Tomorrow you're going to take me back to LL, and keep quiet about it, because if you don't I'll show the video to Brother Jaime ✖ ✖ ✖ ✖ They looked at each other ✖ Looked back at me ✖ ✖ What video? ✖ ✖ ✖ ✖ The one I took of you down Syria Passage on my phone, course ✖ ✖ ✖ ✖ ✖ ✖ They had their backs to Brother Jaime and I could see all three of their faces. On the first two, sheer panic. Behind them the face of a saint ✖ ✖ Before turning around I said, not bothering to keep my voice down: See you tomorrow then, half past eight at the bus station ✖ ✖ ✖ ✖ ✖

And there they were ✖ ✖ Arms crossed, fidgeting ✖ ✖ ✖ They offered me a coffee, we chatted to the driver as he ate an italiano, then we left ✖ ✖ ✖ ✖ On the bus I turned around, buried my chin in the back of the seat, and asked them what they were really planning to do in LL ✖ I added, softly: Make out among the guanacos? Frolic in the hills? ✖ ✖ ✖ ✖ We're here to visit the last few young people left in this town, Sister, replied Josías. The elderly are being left alone, just like everywhere else, and the people you ate with last night look after them, among other things ✖ ✖ ✖ ✖ ✖ Don't they care that the old people are committing idolatry, right there in the church? ✖ That's exactly why we're here: we're going to lift them up, all of them, above that plaster statue of the virgin, answered Bryan. It's only a matter of time before they remember the

Father ✖ But they might've been led astray a long time ago, I replied ✖ There's no swallow that won't take to the wing and head north when the cold sets in, Sister ✖ I reminded them: It is profitable for thee that one of thy members should perish, and not that thy whole body should be cast into hell ✖ Bryan counterattacked: Sometimes you've got to put your neck on the line, sometimes even your soul. Like a lamb that learns to howl in order to survive the winter ✖ I raised my eyebrows, turned around, and tried to sleep for a while. I wasn't in the mood for arguing ✖ ✖ ✖

✖ When I opened my eyes the bus was parked in LL by a roadside shrine, next to a half-built brick wall ✖ ✖ The Saints were watching me worriedly, one beside the other. I wondered how long they'd been trying to figure out where my phone was ✖ ✖ ✖ ✖ Don't bother, I told them, it's right here, where you'd never dare look ✖ Hold your tongue and tell us what you're planning to do, said Josías. Bryan breathed hard through his nose, his jaw like a fist ✖ Let's make a deal, I said: We'll spend however long you need here converting all the old people, and in return you'll come with me to Fray Santiago, to the old machine warehouse, to look for my old man ✖ ✖ They glanced at each other again and asked what papá santo was doing there ✖ That's exactly what I want to know, I replied sadly. It's been ages now since he took off and I don't know what to do ✖ ✖ ✖ Actually, I don't even know if that's where he is ✖ ✖ ✖ I wanted someone to hug me, but the

Brothers, although moved, were still nervous about the video ✖ They held out their hands to me: It's a deal ✖

✖ ✖ ✖ ✖ We were crossing the square toward the Saints' temple when a procession of old women surrounding a priest and a pair of altar boys came out of the church ✖ ✖ The father, dizzy from the heat and the constant pestering, nodded his head all over the place without knowing whom he was agreeing with ✖ ✖ The old women, wearing ribbons and badges to mark their status, leaned in so close when they spoke that they blessed him with their saliva ✖ When the moment came, the altar boys were single-minded: they wrestled their way out to the pickup truck and scattered ✖ ✖ ✖ Until next year ✖ ✖ ✖ The women would dream, cry, dance alone in their houses, waiting for the procession ✖ ✖ At that moment, in the square, as they were saying goodbye to the priest, he met the Brothers' gaze ✖ I imagined an exchange of obscene gestures between the altar boys and Bryan. The sun was high and you had to walk quickly between patches of shade ✖ ✖ ✖ ✖ ✖ ✖

During the day I helped the Saints wash the streets of LL and visit the old people ✖ ✖ ✖ I quickly got the hang of the rhythm and dived right into whatever chores needed doing ✖ We ate a proper lunch and dinner, thanking the Lord in dining rooms full of trembling beings about to give in to their yawns and disperse ✗ ✗ ✗ ✗ We all, obviously, avoided the houses that belonged to the remaining Catholics ✗ Some of the Saints even avoided stepping on the church's shadow ✗ ✗ You didn't need to ask anyone anything to understand that the Mormons wanted to settle in LL for good, to arrange things differently, with fewer Saints' cards and more community gatherings: more games of momias, their eyes shut and arms linked, praying to the Father and the Son for the grandchildren they never got to know, for their children down south, for the health of their dogs ✗ Brothers Bryan and Josías wandered around, directing prayers, flushed with excitement, their necks black with dirt ✗ Occasionally I'd half open an eye and see them in a trance ✗ ✗ ✗ They were the kind of people who actually believe in what they do.

But they arrived late to dinner, after all the praying and whatnot, looking worried ✗ ✗✗ They gave their thanks, but their minds were elsewhere. You could tell by their voices, which sounded watery ✗ ✗ They ate quickly and made their excuses, practically running out of there ✗ ✗ ✗ ✗ ✗ ✗ I was about to stand up and follow them when I felt one of the young women put her hand on my wrist. Smiling, she pointed me toward a room ✗ ✗ ✗ We couldn't find a bed, Sister, but I'm sure you'll be comfortable on the sofa. We left you some blankets

so you don't get cold ✖ ✖ ✖ Anything you need,
I'll be right here with the rest of the Sisters ✖ ✖
✖ I saw them stretch out their sleeping bags and
get ready for bed ✖ The men were already saying
goodnight ✖ ✖ ✖ I went into the room and lay
down to wait ✖ As soon as they turned off the
light in the dining room I put my ear to the door.
When I heard the first snore I put on my shoes and
went out the window ✖ ✖ ✖ ✖ At the bottom
of the hill a couple of lights were moving ✖ ✖ ✖
I ran after them, skirting the houses ✖ ✖ When
I got closer I recognized the voices of Bryan and
Josías ✖ I kept my distance, walking only when
they walked, and tried to listen ✖ ✖ ✖ ✖ ✖ ✖
✖ Every now and then they'd start debating each
other quietly, then get excited, raising their voices
and making the hares run off terrified through the
cactuses. Then they'd fall silent for a while ✖ ✖ ✖

The lights, there one minute, suddenly disappeared
✖ ✖ ✖ ✖ ✖ ✖ ✖ ✖ ✖

As I tried to follow them I came to an improvised
mineshaft, one of those old, shoddily constructed
ones, pitch black ✖ ✖ ✖ I could hear echoes ✖ I
took a deep breath and went in ✖ ✖ ✖ ✖ ✖ ✖ ✖
✖ ✖ I tried to keep my balance and not whack my
head on the stones ✖ ✖ The tunnel sloped down and
there were hardly any supporting beams left ✖ ✖ ✖
✖ I closed my eyes, dizzy from not being able to see
anything, and so, as blind as if I'd had them open,

I descended ✖ ✖ ✖ ✖
For half an hour maybe, I descended ✖ ✖

✖ It probably wasn't that long, but time stopped mattering ✖ ✖ ✖ ✖ ✖
When it seemed like it couldn't possibly go any further down, the tunnel flattened out and allowed me to walk more easily ✖ After a while the tunnel started sloping up again ✖ ✖ ✖ ✖ ✖ Shit, I thought, the Brothers have led me into a trap ✖ And my mind started whirling: maybe they never came down here, maybe as soon as the echoes of my footsteps had faded they threw down a couple of beams so I'd be trapped ✖ ✖ ✖ ✖ ✖ ✖ ✖ ✖
✖ ✖ I started treading more lightly, trying not to provoke a collapse ✖ My chest a wet sponge, my bones worn out ✖ The mine above me ✖ ✖
✖ ✖ ✖ ✖ ✖ ✖ I did eventually come to an exit, though there were no stars and no cactuses: only a cloud, phosphorescent dust, like an aura ✖ I kept climbing, and just as I was resting against one of the beams on the threshold I saw the silhouettes of the Brothers, their backs to me, holding hands ✖ One of them was on his knees ✖   ✖
✖ ✖ In front of them, occupying an alcove with a little hole that opened up to the sky, something was shining
✖ ✖ ✖ ✖ ✖ ✖ ✖ ✖ ✖
✖ ✖ When I saw the x-rays for the first time, 668a reminded me of whatever that shining thing was that day ✖ ✖ ✖ ✖

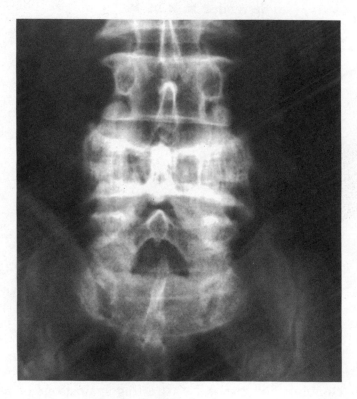

668a

A chariot of light, an angel with four faces, a UFO, a
vertebra straining toward the moon: all empty words
✗ ✗ ✗ ✗ ✗ ✗

Whatever it was stayed there a while and then became
a thread that rose up to the heavens through the little
hole ✗ ✗ ✗ ✗ ✗ In the darkness again, emptiness
reigned ✗ ✗ ✗ The Brothers were weeping, sobbing.

I saw them embracing ✖ ✖ ✖ When they shined a light toward the entrance and saw me I didn't ask them anything. What could they have known?

✖ ✖ ✖ ✖ ✖

✖ ✖ ✖ ✖ ✖
We exited through the mouth of the mine ✖ ✖ ✖ ✖ I took so many breaths of pure air I thought I was going to explode ✖ ✖ ✖ ✖ The Brothers walked on, step after heavy step, drained ✖ ✖ ✖ Not even stopping to get their breath back ✖ ✖ ✖ ✖ I lay down on the ground for a moment, the stars burning my eyelashes, and waited. Ten minutes later I ran to catch up to them ✖ ✖ ✖ ✖ ✖ As soon as I found them they passed me one of the flashlights. I went first, lighting the way ✖ ✖ ✖ ✖ ✖ ✖ ✖ Bryan and Josías dragged their feet behind. Every now and again I heard them sniffling ✖ ✖ ✖ ✖ ✖ But which of them was crying? And why? ✖ ✖ ✖ ✖ ✖ When we arrived at the square I held the light up to their faces and asked what had happened down there ✖ ✖ ✖ ✖ Kolob? murmured Josías, looking at Bryan like he was telling a joke ✖ ✖ ✖ ✖ ✖

KOLOB
        I repeated it to myself, as though memorizing the password to heaven ✖ ✖ ✖ ✖ ✖ ✖ ✖

✖ ✖ ✖ ✖ ✖ KOLOB and a sign: x-ray 668a, the drawings on the hills, the shape of the cliffs, the face

in the mountain seen from the sky ✖ ✖ ✖ ✖ ✖
✖ ✖

The virgencita herself and her tears, the thick fog and
cloud in the valleys ✖ ✖

KOLOB ✖ ✖ ✖
✖ ✖ ✖ ✖ ✖ ✖ ✖ ✖ ✖ ✖ ✖ ✖ ✖ ✖ ✖ ✖ ✖
✖ ✖ ✖ ✖ ✖ ✖ ✖ ✖ ✖ ✖ ✖ ✖ ✖ ✖ ✖ ✖
✖ ✖ ✖ ✖ ✖ ✖ ✖ ✖ ✖ ✖ ✖ ✖ ✖ ✖ ✖ ✖
✖ ✖ ✖ ✖ ✖ ✖ ✖ ✖ ✖ ✖ ✖ ✖ ✖ ✖ ✖ ✖
✖ ✖ ✖ ✖ ✖ ✖ ✖ ✖ ✖ ✖ ✖

The muscles in the Brothers' faces were tense as they
looked at me, noses swollen ✖ ✖ ✖ ✖ Trembling ✖
✖ ✖ They locked themselves in the pickup, turned
on the radio, and talked ✖ ✖ ✖ ✖ ✖ ✖ ✖ Josías
raised his face toward the sky and brought a finger
to his chest, on the left side, where he carried his
Book of Mormon ✖ ✖ ✖ ✖ ✖ Bryan just nodded
and blinked, caressing the steering wheel ✖ ✖ ✖
✖ Every now and then they looked at me ✖ ✖ ✖
✖ Finally they opened one of the back doors and
started the engine ✖ ✖ ✖ ✖ ✖ ✖ ✖ ✖ ✖ ✖ ✖
✖ ✖ ✖ The truck's headlights laid open the desert,
black and compact ✖ ✖ ✖ ✖ ✖ ✖ ✖ ✖ ✖ ✖ ✖
✖ ✖ ✖

We went back to Ch that same night, without saying
anything more ✖ ✖ ✖ ✖ ✖ ✖ ✖ Before getting
out in front of my house, I promised them I'd keep

quiet ✖ ✖ ✖ ✖ They looked at me in the rearview mirror, suspicious ✖ ✖ ✖   ✖ ✖ I realized my words sounded empty, so to try and reconcile things I smashed my phone as they watched ✖ ✖ Their expressions didn't change ✖   ✖   ✖   ✖   ✖ ✖   ✖   ✖   ✖ Maybe they'd even forgotten about the video ✖

      ✖ ✖ ✖ ✖ ✖ ✖

The last thing I remember from that night is lying down on the bed where I used to sleep with papá santo ✖ But I woke up very early the next day in the temple   ✖   ✖   ✖   ✖ Sister Ruth was crouched down, giving me a worried look ✖ ✖ ✖ ✖ ✖ ✖ ✖ ✖ ✖ ✖ ✖ ✖ ✖✖ ✖ ✖ ✖ ✖ ✖ ✖ She offered to buy me a cup of tea and asked if I remembered how I'd gotten there, if anything was wrong ✖ ✖ Is anything right, more like, Sister, I replied. I can't really remember anything from last night ✖ I lowered my eyes and she took me to the café ✖ After a cup of tea we hugged, and she didn't let me go till I promised that if anything happened I would come to her house and get her ✖ How did you find me? I asked at some point, as we sipped from our mugs

      I came in and saw you at the feet of the Prophet, crying in your sleep ✖

I went home to try and get some rest ✖ ✖ ✖ A pain very similar to the one I feel now was undoing me from the inside ✖ ✖ ✖ Like my body was a pile of chicken bones and death a fat glutton sucking on them greedily ✖ ✖ ✖ ✖ But before I'd even started up the stairs I heard a knock at the door ✖ ✖ ✖ ✖ ✖ ✖ ✖ ✖ ✖ ✖ When I looked out, one of the neighbors was staring at her hands like she was trying to erase her fingerprints ✖ We looked straight at each other ✖ One of her eyes was the color of milk ✖ Your papá's not coming back, she said ✖ How do you know for sure? ✖ He hasn't been back since he left. If you're going hungry, mijita, all you have to do is say. She gave a sad sigh and tried to stroke my hair ✖ ✖ ✖ ✖ ✖ I jerked my head back, arching my neck, and shut the door in her face

I don't need your help or anyone else's, I shouted back ✖✖✖✖✖✖✖✖✖✖✖✖✖✖

And he stood between the dead and the living; and
the plague was stayed.
Numbers 16:48

It was because of what happened to Isidorita that I saw the young doctor again ✖ ✖ ✖ ✖ Something was obviously up, because she'd been coming every other day and then disappeared completely ✖ ✖ ✖ ✖ I didn't realize how long I'd been bedbound, laid low by the metastasis, till she appeared in the doorway, smiling, red and shiny and dragging a suitcase ✖ I asked her how she'd been, and she fainted: put one foot in front of the other and fell face-first onto the floor ✖ ✖ ✖ ✖ ✖ ✖ ✖ ✖ I called the doctor ✖ My voice was trembling so much he must have thought: Señora Nancy's on her last legs, I'd better get over there quickly to see her on her way ✖

✖ The doctor almost tripped over the fat woman's body, which was lying there spread-eagled ✖ Looks like she's dying, I told him ✖ ✖ ✖ In truth I didn't think it was anything more than a fever, a cold maybe. But when the doctor set about examinin her properly his faced changed so quickly I thought the poor woman had come precisely so she could drop dead in the place where she was most herself, the place where she felt safe ✖ ✖ ✖ ✖ She has an advanced vaginal infection, he told me, with a look that asked what he should do ✖ Do what you can, I replied. She can stay here with me. There's some cash hidden at the back of the underwear drawer: take what you need, and while you're here stick me with that needle, will you? I can't take it anymore ✖ ✖ ✖ ✖

Of course, he replied, and got on with doing everything he could without further comment ✖ ✖ ✖ ✖ ✖

As the days went by, Isidora got worse. There were nights when I couldn't sleep because of the pain, and I spent them gripping the edge of the bed, wanting to vomit one minute from the cancer and the next from the fat woman's smell.

✖ One morning I asked the doctor to pass me Isidora's suitcase. Inside, apart from a couple of bras and some clothes, was a box full of newspaper clippings and folded posters ✖ ✖ ✖ In amongst them all was a photo of what I thought at first was a sea urchin cracked open ✖ ✖ ✖ Then I looked at it closely, and asked the doctor to read aloud the paragraph preceding the photo, part of the same clipping ✖ ✖ ✖ ✖ ✖ He started reading it quietly to himself first, in the light from the window, but I hurried him

✘ ✘ It's an article about biology, he said, and cleared his throat:

"…'The notion that we are the only miracle in the universe seems increasingly infantile as our knowledge of the world around us advances. Many people, concerned about ghosts or asteroids, do not recognize the fact that we coexist with a realm of microscopic organisms, which, seen up close, never ceases to amaze. Let's take, for example, the fungal kingdom. It has citizens everywhere, all over the world. It is where life and death present us with one of their deepest mysteries,' claims forensic entomologist Stuart Chapman, as we walk through the corridors of the Australian Biodiversity Information Services where he is principal investigator in the field of entomology. 'The fungal kingdom has its own rules and strategies, and it has a sinister capacity for variation. There is a whole branch here that specializes, for example, in infection—in a fungus's violent, deadly occupation of a particular kind of insect. All it takes is for a spore to stick to an insect's exoskeleton and begin to germinate in the moisture: colonization is inevitable, and all that remains is for the visitor and the resident to get to know one another properly. With their nervous system paralyzed, all the host can feel is the guest entering and taking control. Then there is proliferation, flourishing, live geometry. Every host, moreover, provides a particular kind of food for his captor. A biological source in whose most private chamber resides a unique figure, a special mechanic used t generate a set of spores that will eventually go on, via airborne transmission, to settle in another organism. The first question to come to mind is: What is this? What do we call this synthesis arising from infection?' I scratch my head, uncomfortable now that the expert, evidently excited, has fallen silent. I try to think of something to break the ice but it's too late: in the palm of his hand he holds a little glass box containing an insect, completely still, which he himself seems happy to call a 'zombie.' 'When the fungus bursts out from inside this Cordyceps militaris specimen, spilling across the continent, what will happen?'..."

✖ ✖ ✖ When the young doctor finished reading I asked him to show me the photo again ✖ He came over and we looked at it for a while ✖

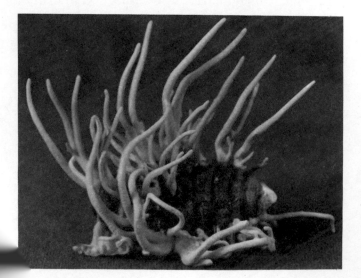

Thanks to Doctor Stuart Chapman I spent an awfully long time, as I looked at the bug-flower in the photo accompanying the article, wondering what on earth it could be.

Isidora improved after a couple of days and stayed to look after me ✖ Until then the smell had made it impossible to go back into that room ✖ ✖ ✖ I kept thinking I'd woken up in the night, gone upstairs, and peered in, half-hidden, to see her panting, leaning against a corner, legs splayed ✖ ✖　✖ ✖ Sometimes I even opened my eyes and thought the house was full of people passing through in procession, lining up all the way from the corner of the street to the bedroom door just to see the fat woman ✖ ✖ I felt like any moment now I'd have to go up and find her turned into a tree or a shrine. Her face barely visible above the clothes rolled right up to her double chin, a couple of quiet indigenous women helping to keep her fat belly out in the open air so the miracle would be visible ✖ ✖

Forty brown-skinned guests in total silence, illuminated by a coral reef: an exquisite forest of tentacles and phosphorescence flowering between Isidorita's thighs ✖ ✖

Obviously what actually happened, contrary to what I dreamed, was that the fat woman was delirious with fever, waking up one day and the next taking a turn for the worse: she couldn't sleep for the pain and would scratch herself all day long, lying there crying, barely able to piss ✖ ✖ Now that she's better, mind you, she's like a sister to me ✖ ✖   ✖ ✖ We while away the hours together, like when Pato and I used to walk along the beach or wait for it to get dark in the empty lot next to our house in Ch ✖

Sparrowhawks of Christ is over but a new telenovela has started: *Prayer Is Not Enough*, in which a boy, who after a huge amount of work managed to get in to study law, abandons it all to follow a French priest as he goes about his community work, the dictatorship raging all the while ✖ Isidorita's whole body quivers with passion every time there's a close-up of the priest delivering some profound revolutionary line ✖ I laugh and ask why she's so trembly ✖ Isn't it a shame priests aren't like that anymore? I swear all the nice, good-looking ones died years ago, she says ✖ ✖ Maybe so, Isidora. I couldn't say ✖ ✖ ✖ ✖ ✖ ✖   ✖   ✖   ✖ I don't believe in curates, or cures for that matter ✖ She always looks at me like a guilty dog and, even though I laugh painfully, I still insist, passing her the envelope full of x-rays: How could I? ✖ ✖ The conversation usually ends there, and we go back to looking at the screen ✖ I'm just seeing blurry silhouettes, really ✖ Isidora watching carefully in case the priest reappears ✖ ✖ If the episode has an improbable ending, the fat woman hugs me excitably and says: You cynic, Nancy! Anything is possible! ✖ And I repeat, quietly, to myself: How am I supposed to believe that if I didn't even believe what I saw with my own eyes ✖ ✖ More than once, on hearing me, she'll ask in return: But what was it that you saw? ✖ ✖ ✖ What did you see, Nancy?

✖ ✖ ✖ And I show her x-ray 668a, held up against the light, and shrug.

Get thee out of thy country, and from thy kindred, and from thy father's house, unto a land that I will shew thee

Genesis 12:1

As I leaned against the door, just back from the temple, waiting for the neighbor to leave the courtyard, all I could think about was seeing papá perdido, hugging him, being with him quietly ✖ My heart was a drum, giving me strength ✖ ✖ ✖ ✖ I had to find the Brothers and make them keep their promise. Make them take me to Fray Santiago as soon as possible ✖ ✖

✖ I walked all around Ch in the morning and then again after lunch, without success ✖ ✖ ✖ The Brothers weren't down by the Syria Passage, nor in the square, nor anywhere near the temple ✖ ✖ ✖ ✖ ✖ It was like they'd been abducted ✖ ✖ ✖ ✖ I grabbed myself an ice cream outside the post office, mulling over the excursion ✖ ✖ ✖ ✖ ✖ ✖ ✖ ✖ ✖ ✖ ✖ That's where I saw him ✖ The Romany ✖ ✖ ✖ ✖ In the back of a pickup, smiling, taking pots and pans to where they always sold them on the outskirts of Ch ✖ ✖ ✖ ✖ I decided to go and

look for him at the crossroads ✖ ✖ ✖ ✖ ✖ ✖ ✖
✖ ✖ ✖ ✖ ✖ And there he was, exactly where I
knew I'd find him ✖ I waved. His cousins looked at
him, smiling ✖ Gorja, he said. What d'you want ✖
I need you to take me to Fray Santiago, I replied. I
need to see my papá ✖ ✖ ✖ ✖ ✖ ✖ ✖ ✖ ✖ ✖ ✖ ✖
✖ ✖ ✖ ✖ ✖ ✖ ✖ ✖ ✖ ✖ ✖ ✖ ✖ ✖ ✖ ✖ ✖ ✖ ✖ ✖
✖ ✖ Jesulé gave me a look so furious I thought he
might fly at me ✖ I went closer and implored him:
Please, it's the last thing I'll ask you for ✖ 'Fraid we're
shooting straight for Bolivia, paisa. Besides, waste of
gas dropping you there ✖ ✖ ✖ ✖ I've got money,
I told him, showing him what I had left from selling
the car ✖ He smiled at me, tucked away the notes,
and said: Get your stuff and we'll go. We leave in
two hours ✖ ✖ ✖ He went off whistling, happy to
have money back in his pocket ✖ ✖ But how could
he care about money now. I didn't ✖ ✖ ✖ I needed
to see papá santo as soon as possible ✖ ✖ ✖ ✖ ✖
✖ ✖ ✖ I went home, made some sandwiches and
a thermos of coffee and chucked some clothes in a
backpack, determined to stay with him a couple of
days. If I could find him, that is.

✖ Maybe Fray Santiago's brainwashed him, I
thought, and now he can live calmly in the Kingdom
of God ✖

✖✖✖✖✖✖✖✖✖✖✖✖✖✖✖✖✖✖✖✖✖✖✖
✖✖✖✖✖✖✖✖✖✖✖✖✖✖✖✖✖✖✖✖✖✖✖

✗ ✗ ✗ ✗ ✗ ✗ We headed for the abandoned salt mine in the middle of the afternoon, at the head of a huge convoy ✗ ✗ ✗ ✗ ✗ ✗ In the distance we saw the sun reflecting off cars at a standstill in the road ✗ ✗ ✗ When we reached them we stopped ✗ Jesulé swore loudly ✗ He walked back to the rest of the convoy, which had parked alongside the highway, and argued with everyone ✗ ✗ ✗ When after a while he returned I didn't know if he was more angry with me or with his paisas. He promised me: We'll get you to your old man, kid, don't you worry ✗ ✗ ✗ With a jerk of the gearshift he headed into the pampa, parallel to the line of stationary cars: we sliced through the hawthorn and sent rocks flying. Didn't stop till we got there ✗ ✗ ✗ A couple of pickups from the convoy followed behind ✗ ✗ ✗ ✗ ✗ ✗ ✗ The salt mine was full of people ✗ ✗ Full ✗ I asked him to wait for me a while ✗ He said that wasn't the deal, they were all rushing to get to the Bolivian border before dark ✗ I ignored him and ran off to look for my papá, leaving everything in the pickup ✗ ✗

✗ ✗ Jesulé's cousins smoked and stretched their legs ✗ ✗ ✗ ✗ ✗ ✗

I searched every face but there was no sign of my old man ✗ Everyone was decked out like they were heading to mass ✗ ✗ ✗ ✗ That is: they were dancing on the dirt roads, the men looking sharp, the women in dresses, like a parody of what the guru had tried to capture in his film ✖ There was a pickup on every corner, all of them playing the same kind of music rescued from scratched vinyl, and people were going crazy: flicking their wrists, swinging their necks and calves to the sound of the Charleston ✖ ✖ ✖ Laughter ✖ ✖ ✖ Bending their legs and arms like puppets.

✖ ✖ ✖ ✖ ✖ ✖ ✖ ✖ Dizzy from the sun, brushed off by everyone I spoke to, I told myself: I'm not leaving here alive without him. And it wasn't till I was breathless, agitated, thinking about going back, that I saw a dog come out of the door to a warehouse ✖ ✖ ✖ ✖ I went in and there he was ✖ Lying on a cot with a cigarette in his mouth, staring at the sky through the roof beams ✖ ✖ ✖ ✖ ✖ ✖ ✖ ✖ He barely registered my hello ✖ Papá, I said, I've come to see you ✖ ✖ ✖ ✖ ✖ ✖ ✖ ✖ ✖ ✖ ✖ ✖ Met with silence, I tried again, and again: Papá, I've come to see you ✖ ✖ ✖ ✖ ✖ ✖ But he didn't answer ✖ ✖ ✖ Didn't even bother to look at me ✖ ✖ ✖ Nothing

✖ ✖ ✖ ✖ ✖ ✖ I left the thermos of coffee and the sandwiches on the floor ✖ ✖ ✖ Don't you trouble yourself, sir, I yelled: Sure, there's an infernal dance going on in the graveyard out there but the only one holy water can't save is you ✖ ✖ ✖ ✖

I thought about giving up on the whole damn thing, but as I left the warehouse my muscles started swelling, and I barely managed to reach a cheerful old

couple walking by, dressed to the nines, before col-
lapsing onto them ✖ They peered into my face, their
mouths moving. They looked like they were made of
wax ✖ ✖ ✖ I sat down for a while in the shade and
watched how people continued to wander, despite
the sun going down and the buses no longer playing
music, stretching their legs, laughing, taking down
their umbrellas and parasols, running their fingers
around their hats, dusting off their dresses with open
palms ✖ ✖ Jesulé appeared around the corner and
gave me a questioning look ✖ I can't leave yet, I
told him ✖ He spat and made a squeaking noise
with his teeth ✖ ✖ I gotta do a second run, he said:
Gimme a week and I'll come get you, same spot ✖
Before he left he brought my backpack and a couple
of blankets from the truck ✖ ✖ ✖ To sleep in, so
you don't get soaked, paisa ✖ ✖ ✖ ✖ ✖ ✖ ✖
✖ ✖ ✖ ✖ ✖ ✖ ✖ ✖ ✖ ✖ ✖ ✖ ✖ ✖
✖ ✖ ✖ ✖ ✖ ✖ ✖ ✖ ✖ ✖ ✖ ✖ ✖ ✖
✖ ✖ ✖ ✖ ✖ ✖ ✖ ✖

I took advantage of the residual daylight to go to the
cemetery of crosses, where we'd dug up my grandfather ✖ ✖ The tips of the hills were flaming pink.
Below, a line sliced the pampa in two, plowing through
the crosses to the warehouse's adobe walls ✖ ✖ ✖
✖ ✖ ✖ The same line bisected me diagonally: top
half salmon pink, bottom half dark blue ✖✖ ✖✖
✖✖✖ Some dogs were sleeping up against one of
the walls ✖ ✖ Then the crosses appeared ✖ All those
crosses ✖ ✖ ✖ ✖ ✖ ✖ And in the distance rusty

machinery ✖ ✖ Fossils of the future ✖ ✖ ✖ ✖
✖ ✖ ✖ ✖ ✖ ✖ In front of my grandfather's cross
the grave was covered over as we'd left it ✖ ✖ Next
to it was a new cross, made of young wood ✖ ✖ ✖
Leaning on top of a little mound of fresh earth ✖ ✖
✖ ✖ The inscription on the wood said:

✖ ✖ ✖ ✖ ✖ ✖ ✖ ✖ ✖ ✖ ✖ ✖ ✖ ✖ ✖ ✖ ✖ ✖ ✖

𝔓𝔞𝔱𝔯𝔦𝔠𝔦𝔬 𝔐𝔬𝔦𝔰é𝔰 ℭ𝔬𝔯𝔱é𝔰 𝔄𝔯𝔞𝔶𝔞
𝔖𝔬𝔫, 𝔟𝔯𝔬𝔱𝔥𝔢𝔯, 𝔞𝔫𝔡 𝔣𝔯𝔦𝔢𝔫𝔡
1997 − 2016

✖ ✖ ✖ ✖ ✖ ✖ ✖ ✖ ✖ ✖ ✖ ✖ ✖ ✖ ✖ ✖ ✖ ✖ ✖

My heart stopped and I sat down for a moment ✖ ✖

✖ Papá santo had found him ✖ ✖ ✖

✖ ✖ ✖ ✖ ✖ ✖ ✖ ✖ ✖ ✖ ✖ ✖ ✖ ✖ ✖ ✖ ✖ ✖ ✖
✖ ✖ ✖ ✖ ✖ ✖ ✖ ✖ ✖ ✖ ✖ ✖ ✖ ✖ ✖ ✖ ✖ ✖ ✖
✖ ✖ ✖ ✖ ✖ ✖ ✖ ✖ ✖ ✖ ✖ ✖ ✖ ✖ ✖ ✖ ✖ ✖ ✖

I stuck my head inside the tin door and there he was,
just as I'd left him: illuminated by a gas lamp, staring
at the ceiling, at the beams, at the huge shadows cast
by insects on the walls ✖ ✖ ✖ ✖ ✖ ✖ ✖ ✖ ✖
✖ I picked up the sandwiches and the thermos of
coffee and sat down on the edge of the bed ✖ ✖ ✖
✖ ✖ ✖ ✖ How long's it been since you ate? I asked
him as I split one of the rolls in two. I left half of it

on his belly, which rose and fell gently ✖ ✖ ✖ Papá santo looked at me, his face contorted, sucking in his cheeks ✖ ✖ ✖ ✖ ✖ I tried to wash down the turkey mayo with a gulp of coffee but between my tongue and my belly button there was nothing but anxiety ✖ ✖ ✖ ✖ ✖ I cleared my throat and went for it:

And how long's it been since you found Pato? ✖ ✖ ✖ ✖ ✖ ✖ Papá santo looked at me like I'd twisted his soul and replied, roughly:

I told you that good-for-nothing's beyond saving, what are you talking about, Nancy ✖

✖ ✖ I pressed him: I asked how long it's been since you found him, not since you saved him ✖

✖ All I found was a hand, he said ✖ ✖ ✖ ✖ ✖ ✖ That and the leather jacket he had on that day. You wanna know where?

The hand in the dump at San Fermín, but it was the cops who left it there, probably wasn't even Pato's ✖ ✖ ✖ Only found out 'cause a bunch of mutants did me a favor ✖ ✖

✖ The jacket in Playa Verde, where that river of shit from San Fermín empties out into the sea ✖ ✖ ✖ ✖ ✖ ✖ ✖ ✖

✖ And the rest of him? ✖ ✖

✖ ✖ Fuck the rest of him ✖ ✖ Who knows what he was mixed up in, or why he ended up there ✖ ✖ ✖ ✖ ✖ ✖ ✖ ✖ The hand was black, hard

✖ ✖ ✖ ✖ ✖ ✖ ✖ ✖ The jacket looked like it was about to grow legs and run off ✖ ✖

✖　✖✖　✖✖　✖✖　✖✖　✖✖　✖✖　✖✖　✖✖　✖✖
✖✖　✖✖　✖✖　✖✖　✖✖　✖✖　✖✖　✖　✖✖　✖✖
✖✖　✖✖　✖✖　✖✖　✖✖　✖✖　✖✖　✖
✖　✖✖　✖✖　✖✖　✖✖　　　　　　✖　✖✖　✖✖
✖　　　　　　✖　✖✖　✖
✖　✖✖　✖✖　✖✖　✖✖　✖✖　✖✖　✖✖　✖✖

Isidora loves this story ✖ ✖ ✖ ✖ ✖ ✖ ✖ Whenever we don't have much to talk about she'll ask me to tell it again: How was it they found Pato, Nancy? ✖ They never found him, I reply ✖ ✖ ✖ ✖ ✖ ✖ ✖ ✖ Only that hand and the jacket ✖ ✖ ✖ Though if you ask me, I reckon, and so does papá santo, that hand could have been anyone's ✖ ✖ ✖ And the jacket too ✖ ✖ ✖ ✖ ✖ ✖ ✖ ✖ ✖ ✖ ✖
✖ ✖ ✖ ✖ ✖
✖ ✖ ✖ ✖ ✖

✖ ✖ ✖ ✖ This is what my papá said, I tell the fat woman then:

✖ ✖ This cop came to see me on the film set to tell me they'd pretty much figured out Pato's where-abouts ✖ He's alive then, I replied, but he looked at me strangely and said no, he'd tell me on the way ✖ But we got all the way to San Fermín without him opening his mouth ✖ ✖ ✖ ✖ ✖

✖ ✖ Outside the city, at the municipal landfill, there were two forensics trucks ✖ ✖ ✖ ✖ ✖ ✖ ✖

✖ ✖ We walked across a mound of debris and trash to a remote area cordoned off with security tape ✖ Surrounding the place were thin, gray kids, some of their stomachs swollen, belly buttons popping ✖ ✖ ✖ There were TV reporters there too, and a bunch of fat neighbors wearing slippers, smoking and talking ✖ ✖ ✖ ✖ Black clouds to the north ✖ ✖ ✖ Black clouds to the south

✖ ✖ ✖ ✖ ✖ The two coal plants operating perfectly ✖ ✖ ✖ ✖ ✖

✖ I was greeted by four cops, slick and serious, hiding behind dark glasses ✖ ✖ ✖ Deputy Chief Calderón, that's what the one who came to get me was called, cleared his throat and said: 'Fraid I've not been completely straight with you, Pastor ✖ ✖ ✖ The investigation's come a long way but we've only found a hand and a jacket ✖ We'll need you to identify them ✖ ✖ ✖ ✖ ✖ ✖ ✖ He indicated a forensics van and I went in ✖ On the table was what I thought was a monkey's hand ✖ ✖ ✖ Black and wrinkled ✖ ✖ ✖ ✖ No thumb ✖ ✖ ✖ ✖ Next to it was an open jar. It smelled like a morgue ✖ ✖ ✖ ✖ I managed to say, just to placate everyone: Yes, it's Pato's ✖ And I tried to cry. I mean: I cried, but I didn't really want to ✖ ✖ ✖ ✖ That little piece of meat could have belonged to anything ✖ ✖ ✖ ✖
✖ ✖ ✖ ✖ ✖ ✖ ✖ ✖ ✖ ✖ ✖ ✖ ✖ ✖ ✖ ✖ ✖ ✖
✖ ✖ ✖ ✖ ✖ ✖ ✖ ✖ ✖ ✖ ✖ ✖ ✖ ✖ ✖ ✖ ✖ ✖
✖ ✖ ✖ ✖ ✖ ✖ ✖ ✖ ✖ ✖ ✖ ✖ ✖ ✖ ✖ ✖ ✖ ✖
✖ ✖ ✖ ✖ ✖ ✖ ✖ ✖ ✖ ✖ ✖ ✖ ✖ ✖ ✖ ✖ ✖ ✖
✖ ✖ ✖ ✖ ✖ ✖ ✖ ✖ ✖ ✖ ✖ ✖ ✖ ✖ ✖ ✖ ✖ ✖

✖ But I wanted some peace, and for them to leave me be ✖ ✖ ✖ ✖ I had a moment alone in the fenced-off area and took the opportunity to sit down for a smoke ✖ ✖ ✖ A couple of kids whistled at me from the other side of the barrier ✖ ✖ ✖ ✖ ✖ They had hard black eyes, like the monkey hand ✖ ✖ ✖ I don't have any money, I told them, and this is my last cigarette: shove off, won't you ✖ ✖ The tallest one smiled, his maw empty except for two sharp eyeteeth. Don't let 'em fool you, sir ✖ ✖

✖ Pato's alive ✖   ✖   ✖ ✖ ✖ ✖ ✖ ✖ ✖ He's living near here ✖ ✖ ✖ ✖ ✖ ✖ ✖ ✖ ✖ ✖ ✖ ✖ ✖ ✖ ✖ ✖ ✖ ✖ ✖

I asked them where but they rubbed their fingers in my face ✖ ✖ For ten lucas they'd even bring me Pato's real hand ✖ I gave them the money and they came back within five minutes with a shoe box ✖ ✖ You'll keep this quiet, Pastor, they told me. We don't want any trouble from the fuzz ✖ ✖ ✖ ✖ ✖ ✖ ✖ ✖ ✖ ✖ ✖ ✖ ✖ ✖ ✖ ✖ So where's Pato then? I asked them. And why's he missing a hand? Where

the fuck did you brats even get this? ✖ ✖ ✖ ✖ ✖
✖ ✖ ✖ ✖ ✖ ✖ There were five or six of them ✖
They looked at each other, trying not to laugh ✖ ✖
✖ ✖ ✖ Just then the Deputy Chief Calderón blew
a whistle: I saw him signaling that it was time to go.
When I looked back the kids had scattered, running
over the landfill site ✖ ✖ ✖ ✖ ✖ ✖ ✖ ✖ ✖ It
was probably just some lie to get money out of me
✖ ✖ ✖ I grabbed the box, not daring to look inside
✖ ✖ Calderón didn't ask me anything, either about
the box or the kids. He seemed very respectful of the
pain in my face, and so we kept quiet, listening to the
radio, until he took a detour toward the coast ✖ ✖
✖ ✖ ✖ ✖ ✖ ✖ ✖ ✖ ✖ ✖ ✖ ✖ ✖ Where are
you taking me now? I asked ✖

✖ ✖ To the other place, where the jacket is ✖ ✖ ✖
✖ ✖ ✖ ✖ Forty-five minutes later we were on the
fetid blue sand of Playa Verde ✖ ✖ ✖ A couple of
forensics trucks were parked by the cordoned-off area
✖ ✖ ✖ ✖ ✖ ✖ ✖ The wind gusted strongly ✖ ✖
✖ ✖ I walked blindly, my head half-buried in my
jacket, lips pressed shut so the whirls of black, green,
and gold pyrite dust wouldn't get in my mouth ✖ ✖
✖ ✖ ✖ ✖ ✖ ✖ In the distance, the cops were
waiting by the canal ✖ ✖ The beach was a mess,
strewn with trash as though it was winter and the
sea had vomited ✖ ✖ ✖ Tree trunks, bottles, plastic
buoys, and nets ✖ ✖ ✖ ✖ All polished patiently by
the waves, hija ✖ ✖ ✖ ✖ ✖ ✖ ✖ ✖ ✖ ✖ ✖ ✖
Time's relentless in that sense, Nancy, papá santo had

said to me: That farmhand, your tío Aarón's friend, Juan García, he was a sinner same as Pato ✖ ✖ The two of them sentenced to be polished by the water, shredded by the current ✖ ✖ ✖ ✖ ✖ ✖ ✖ ✖ ✖ ✖ ✖ ✖ ✖ Maybe that jacket, the only thing left of him, maybe it was a way of confirming his disappearance from this world ✖ ✖ ✖ ✖ His dissolution ✖ ✖ ✖ ✖ ✖ ✖ ✖ ✖ ✖ Because I did recognize the jacket with the cops that afternoon: it wasn't Pato's but he was wearing one just like it that day ✖ ✖ ✖ Don't you remember? ✖ ✖ ✖ One of the detectives held it up with a stick. Legs splayed, one on either side of the canal ✖ ✖ ✖ ✖ ✖ The jacket had gotten caught up against a pile of trash and was obstructing the flow ✖ ✖ ✖ ✖ ✖ ✖ ✖ ✖ ✖ ✖ ✖ ✖ Yes, it's his, I told them ✖ ✖ ✖ Then I turned around and went to lock myself in the car and smoke ✖ ✖ ✖

When Calderón was about to take the turnoff toward the film set I asked him to leave me in Fray Santiago instead ✖ ✖ ✖ ✖ ✖ ✖ ✖ ✖ ✖ What do you want to go there for, Pastor? ✖ ✖ ✖ ✖ ✖ ✖ ✖ ✖ ✖ ✖ ✖ I'm going to spend some time with my old man ✖ ✖ ✖ ✖ ✖ ✖ ✖ He dropped me off here ✖ ✖ ✖ I gave him the keys to the truck and asked him if he could send someone to pick it up and park it outside the house back in Ch ✖ ✖ ✖ ✖ ✖ Asked if they could let you know ✖ ✖ ✖ ✖ ✖ ✖ ✖ ✖ ✖ ✖ ✖ ✖ ✖ ✖ It was getting dark by the time the car disappeared down the road toward the Panamerican Highway ✖ ✖ ✖ I dug a hole next to my old man's

grave, sat on the ground, and opened the box ✘ ✘
✘ ✘ Inside was a fucked-up pigeon, almost flesh-
less: just a smash of feathers ✘ ✘ ✘ ✘ I buried it
anyway ✘ ✘ ✘ The next day I found some sticks
inside the old warehouse and made Patito a cross
✘ ✘ ✘ ✘ ✘ ✘ ✘ ✘ ✘ ✘ ✘ ✘ ✘ ✘ ✘ ✘ ✘ ✘
✘ ✘ ✘ ✘ ✘ ✘ ✘ ✘ ✘ ✘ ✘ ✘ ✘ ✘ ✘ ✘ ✘ ✘
✘ ✘ ✘ ✘ ✘ ✘ ✘ ✘ ✘ Better we let him rest in
peace, hija, and give ourselves some peace as well ✘
✘ ✘ You have to believe it's possible, even if just for
a little each day   ✘ ✘ ✘

✘ ✘ By the time I got to that part of the story
Isidora would already have her head in my lap, her
lips pressed together ✘ ✘ ✘ ✘ And when my papá
told me and got to that part, I was lying beside him,
looking at all the white, prickly hairs on his neck and
chin, shivering like a field of cactuses ✘ ✘ ✘ ✘
✘ ✘ ✘ ✘ ✘ ✘ And we fell asleep, me in the old
warehouse, Isidora on the bed in this house in the
big port ✘ ✘ ✘ ✘ ✘ ✘ Papá santo was left, eyes
open, staring at me.

✘   ✘   ✘

✘ ✘ ✘ ✘ ✘ ✘ We spent a few quiet days together,
talking as little as possible ✘ ✘ ✘ ✘ ✘ ✘ ✘ ✘ ✘
✘ ✘ In the mornings and when the sun was setting
we'd go out walking ✘ ✘ ✘ ✘ ✘ ✘ ✘ ✘ The rest
of the day we stayed in the warehouse ✘ ✘ ✘ Me
thinking or doing the puzzles in the newspapers I'd

found ✖ ✖ ✖ Papá reading the New Testament or looking around vaguely, stroking the dogs ✖ ✖ ✖ ✖ ✖ ✖

On the second to last day papá appeared in the warehouse carrying two buckets and said: Come with me to water the plants ✖ ✖ ✖ ✖ ✖ We went to the pump and I leaned my whole body weight on the handle, seesawing ✖ ✖ ✖ ✖ After a while a clear stream emerged ✖ ✖ ✖ The dogs jumped around excitedly, passing underneath the stream of water with their mouths open ✖ ✖ As for papá desierto, my desolate father, I think that might be the happiest I ever saw him ✖ ✖ ✖ ✖ He rested a hand on my shoulder and on his face there formed a smile ✖ ✖ ✖ ✖ ✖ ✖ I felt his palm resting on me and it was as though I was carrying him in my arms ✖ ✖ ✖ ✖ ✖

We walked beyond the crosses, behind the rusty machinery ✖ ✖ ✖ ✖ ✖ ✖ Planks of wood marked out an area where some sun-golden bushes were struggling to stay upright ✖ ✖ ✖ ✖

Nothing grows here, he said ✖ Everything burns from sheer abundance

✖ ✖ ✖ ✖ ✖ So much salt ✖ ✖ ✖ ✖ ✖

When we finished watering we sat there, watching the sun disappear ✖ ✖ ✖ ✖ When the sky went black, that moonless day, the plants began to glimmer, some of them blue, others red ✖ ✖ ✖ ✖ A couple of them green ✖ ✖ ✖ ✖ ✖ ✖ I looked at papá and saw him smile again ✖ ✖ ✖ ✖ I fell asleep with the plants reflecting against my eyelids, as if closing my eyes made the whole universe appear in front of me. Everything that's visible and everything that's not ✖ ✖ ✖ ✖ ✖ ✖ ✖ ✖ I woke up in the warehouse ✖ ✖ ✖ That sunset ✖ The phosphorescent bushes, my father's smile, the whole day ✖ I never knew if I actually lived them, or invented them, or dreamed them, or a bit of all three

✗ ✗ ✗ ✗ ✗ ✗ ✗ ✗ ✗ ✗ ✗ ✗ ✗ ✗ ✗ ✗ ✗
✗ ✗ ✗ ✗ ✗ ✗ ✗ ✗ ✗ ✗ ✗ ✗ ✗ ✗ ✗ ✗ ✗
✗ ✗ ✗ ✗ ✗ ✗ ✗ ✗ ✗ ✗ ✗ ✗ ✗ ✗ ✗ ✗ ✗
✗ ✗ ✗ ✗ ✗ ✗ ✗ ✗ ✗ ✗ ✗ ✗ ✗ ✗ ✗ ✗ ✗
✗ I do remember, definitely, falling asleep again
and dreaming ✗ ✗ ✗ ✗ ✗ ✗ ✗ ✗ ✗ ✗ ✗ ✗ ✗ ✗
✗ that I was sinking ✗ ✗ ✗ ✗ ✗ ✗ ✗ ✗ ✗ ✗ ✗
✗ ✗ ✗ ✗ ✗ into the crook of his arm ✗ ✗ ✗ ✗
✗ ✗ ✗ ✗ passing through the mattress ✗ ✗ ✗
✗ ✗ ✗ ✗ ✗ ✗ ✗ on and on ✗ ✗ ✗ ✗ ✗ ✗
✗ ✗ ✗ ✗ ✗ face down ✗ ✗ ✗ ✗ ✗ ✗ ✗ ✗
✗ ✗ ✗ through the earth ✗ ✗ ✗ ✗ ✗ ✗ ✗ ✗
✗ ✗ ✗ ✗ ✗ ✗ the pores in the saltpeter ✗ ✗ ✗
✗ ✗ ✗ ✗ ✗ ✗ between ✗ ✗ ✗ ✗ ✗ ✗ ✗ ✗
✗ ✗ ✗ fossilized ✗ ✗ ✗ roots ✗ ✗ ✗ ✗ ✗ ✗
✗ ✗ ✗ ✗ bodies curled up inside blankets ✗ ✗ ✗
✗ ✗ ✗ ✗ ✗ ✗ ✗ bones ✗ ✗ ✗ ✗ ✗ ✗ ✗
✗ ✗ ✗ ✗ ✗ of mylodons ✗ ✗ ✗ in which ✗ ✗
✗ ✗ ✗ ✗ ✗ ✗ treasures were blossoming ✗ ✗
✗ ✗ ✗ ✗ jungles of quartz and Spanish glass ✗
✗ ✗ ✗ ✗ ✗ ✗ as though the earth ✗ ✗ ✗ ✗ ✗
✗ ✗ ✗ ✗ ✗ ✗ ✗ ✗ ✗ was slowly ✗ ✗ ✗ ✗
✗ ✗ ✗ ✗ ✗ ✗ ✗ ✗ ✗ ✗ letting me ✗ ✗ ✗
✗ ✗ ✗ ✗ ✗ ✗ ✗ ✗ ✗ ✗ ✗ ✗ ✗ ✗ in ✗ ✗
✗ ✗ ✗ ✗ ✗ ✗ ✗ ✗ ✗ ✗ ✗ ✗ ✗ ✗ ✗ ✗ ✗
✗ ✗ ✗ ✗ ✗ ✗ ✗ ✗ ✗ ✗ ✗ ✗ ✗ ✗ ✗ ✗ ✗
✗ ✗ ✗ ✗ ✗ ✗ ✗ ✗ ✗ ✗ ✗ ✗ ✗ ✗ ✗ ✗ ✗
✗ ✗ ✗ ✗ ✗ ✗ ✗ ✗ ✗ ✗ ✗ ✗ ✗ ✗ ✗ ✗ ✗
✗ ✗ ✗ ✗ ✗ ✗ ✗ ✗ ✗ ✗ ✗ ✗ ✗ ✗ ✗ ✗
✗ ✗ ✗ ✗ ✗ ✗
✗ ✗ ✗ ✗ ✗ ✗ ✗ ✗ ✗ ✗ ✗ ✗ ✗ ✗

The day before Jesulé came back we said everything that needed to be said. We repeated the same conversation with different words ✕ Four, five, six, seven times ✕ ✕

✕ ✕

✕ ✕ ✕ ✕ ✕ ✕ ✕ I'm leaving, papá, for good, I told him in the end ✕ ✕ ✕ ✕ He looked at me with the eyes of a sacrificial lamb, and sighed:

Do what you have to, Nancy, you're old enough now ✕ ✕ ✕

✕ ✕ I asked myself: Am I old enough? Old enough for what? And changed the subject ✕ ✕ ✕ ✕ ✕ ✕ ✕ ✕ ✕ We laughed a couple of times ✕ ✕ ✕ And talked about my mamá ✕ ✕ I told him in detail what I'd seen that time I'd spent in the big port ✕ ✕ We hugged, too, forgiving her, hoping the woman might be happy one day, preferably far away from the miner ✕ ✕ ✕ ✕

It was possible to say: I love you so much ✕ ✕ ✕ Even the dogs were scrabbling between our feet at the edge of the bed, happy ✕ ✕

✕ There were smiles and peace among the lambs ✕ ✕ ✕ ✕ ✕ ✕ ✕ ✕ ✕ ✕

✕ ✕

And one morning the horn sounded ✘ ✘ ✘ ✘
✘ ✘ I gave him a long hug, and just said

    they've come for me,
    see you ✘ ✘

✘ ✘ ✘ ✘ He heaved a sigh and turned his face to
the wall ✘ ✘ ✘

And I never saw him again ✘ ✘

When I crossed the road I was blinded for a moment:
the white sky was watching over us

I felt Fray Santiago's dogs come closer

Seven growling trucks with their high beams on,
waiting outside the door to the warehouse
✘✘✘✘✘✘✘✘✘✘✘✘✘✘✘✘✘✘✘✘✘✘✘
✘✘✘✘✘✘✘✘✘✘✘✘✘✘✘✘✘✘✘✘
✘✘

        And so it went

✘✘✘✘✘✘✘✘✘✘✘✘✘✘✘✘✘✘✘✘✘✘✘
✘✘✘✘✘✘✘✘✘✘✘✘✘✘✘✘✘✘✘✘✘✘✘
✘✘✘✘✘✘✘✘✘✘✘✘✘✘✘✘✘✘✘✘✘✘✘
✘✘✘✘✘✘✘✘✘✘✘✘✘✘✘✘✘✘✘✘✘✘✘
✘✘✘✘✘✘✘✘✘✘✘✘✘✘✘✘✘✘✘✘✘✘✘
✘✘✘✘✘✘✘✘✘✘✘✘✘✘✘✘✘✘✘✘✘✘✘

xxxxxxxxxxxxxxxxxxxxxxxx
xxxxxxxxxxxxxxxxxxxxxxxx
xxxxxxxxxxxxxxxxxxxxxxxx
xxxxxxxxxxxxxxxxxxxxxxxx
xxxxxxxxxxxxxxxxxxxxxxxx
xxxxxxxxxxxxxxxxxxxxxxxx
xxxxxxxxxxxxxxxxxxxxxxxx
xxxxxxxxxxxxxxxxxxxxxxxx
xxxxxxxxxxxxxxxxxxxxxxxx
xxxxxxxxxxxxxxxxxxxxxxxx
xxxxxxxxxxxxxxxxxxxxxxxx
xxxxxxxxxxxxxxxxxxxxxxxx
xxxxxxxxxxxxxxxxxxxxxxxx
xxxxxxxxxxxxxxxxxxxxxxxx
xxxxxxxxxxxxxxxxxxxxxxxx
xxxxxxxxxxxxxxxxxxxxxxxx
xxxxxxxxxxxxxxxxxxxxxxxx
xxxxxxxxxxxxxxxxxxxxxxxx
xxxxxxxxxxxxxxxxxxxxxxxx
xxxxxxxxxxxxxxxxxxxxxxxx
xxxxxxxxxxxxxxxxxxxxxxxx
xxxxxxxxxxxxxxxxxxxxxxxx
xxxxxxxxxxxxxxxxxxxxxxxx
xxxxxxxxxxxxxxxxxxxxxxxx
xxxxxxxxxxxxxxxxxxxxxxxx
xxxxxxxxxxxxxxxxxxxxxxxx
xxxxxxxxxxxxxxxxxxxxxxxx
xxxxxxxxxxxxxxxxxxxxxxxx
xxxxxxxxxxxxxxxxxxxxxxxx
xxxxxxxxxxxxxxxxxxxxxxxx

XXXXXXXXXXXXXXXXXXXXXXXXX
XXXXXXXXXXXXXXXXXXXXXXXXX
XXXXXXXXXXXXXXXXXXXXXXXXX
XXXXXXXXXXXXXXXXXXXXXXXXX
XXXXXXXXXXXXXXXXXXXXXXXXX
　XXXXXXXXXXXXXXXXXXXX
　　XXXXXXXXXXXXXXXXXX
　　　XXXXXXXXXXXXXX
　　　　XXXXXXXXXXX
　　　　　XXXXXXX
　　　　　　XXXXX
　　　　　　XXX
　　　　　　XX
　　　　　　X

　　　　　　X

　　　　　　X
　　　　　　XX
　　　　　　XXX
　　　　　XXXXX
　　　　XXXXXXX
　　　XXXXXXXXX
　　XXXXXXXXXXXX
　　XXXXXXXXXXXXXX
　XXXXXXXXXXXXXXXXX
XXXXXXXXXXXXXXXXXXXXXXXX
XXXXXXXXXXXXXXXXXXXXXXXX
XXXXXXXXXXXXXXXXXXXXXXXX
XXXXXXXXXXXXXXXXXXXXXXXX
XXXXXXXXXXXXXXXXXXXXXXXX

BRUNO LLORET was born in Santiago, Chile, in 1990. *Nancy*, his debut novel, was highly commended in the Roberto Bolaño Prize, and he published his second novel, *Leña,* in 2018. He currently lives in London.

ELLEN JONES is a researcher, editor, and translator from Spanish, currently based in Mexico City. Her translation of Rodrigo Fuentes's short story collection *Trout, Belly Up* (Charco Press) was shortlisted for the Translators Association First Translation Prize in 2019.